BROKEN FANG

Their bodies crashed together

BROKEN FANG

By

R. G. MONTGOMERY

Illustrations by
LYNN BOGUE HUNT

Caxton Classics

Park Ave. Library
Aztec, NM

CAXTON PRESS
Caldwell, Idaho
2001

Printed and bound in the United States of America
CAXTON PRESS
166836

To
Earl Kirk Montgomery
His First Book

TABLE OF CONTENTS

LIST OF ILLUSTRATIONS

FOREWORD

By Albert Payson Terhune

MOST people like dogs—and know nothing about them. A tiny minority of mankind dislike dogs—and know nothing about them. Thus the average dog story or dog book is written either by someone who knows dogs, but does not know how to write; or else by someone who can write well, but knows pitifully little about his subject.

That is why the authors of genuinely good dog stories can be numbered on the fingers of one hand. The combination of dog-lore and literary-lore is hard to find, as several thousand aspiring scribblers have learned to their puzzled sorrow since such tales came into vogue.

An author who not only knows dogs, but who can make his readers see in the hero of the tale the fine or lovable or whimsical traits of their own dogs has a ready and eager following.

Such a man, most emphatically, is the author of *Broken Fang*.

He knows more than dogs. He knows the mountainous cow-country. He knows it, not synthetically, but as a Long Island commuter knows his instalment-payment home. He has dwelt there and toiled there long enough for the cruel beauty of wilderness life to seep into his very brain and thence undiluted into his book. Here is no dude-ranch-bred smattering of local color; but the work of a man to whom the forests and trackless hills have whispered their grimly gripping secrets. His scenic setting is more than a mere background. It is stark drama by itself.

His hero is Bart, a "breed" dog. In less technical phrase, a wilderness dog whose ancestry has a persistent strain of wolf-blood in it; a dog whose milder canine traits are so mixed with the lupine urge that his hold on civilized life is tenuous. Ever, in his gallant heart, the call of the wilderness and of its furtive, gray denizens is battling with his inherent loyalty to his "breed" master and with his duties as range-guard.

Here, too, is another of the many lures of *Broken Fang*. Is there one of us, who, soon or late, has not heard, however faintly, the mystic summons to cast aside our stiff white-collar civilization and to return to the life which once our forest forebears led?

For the most part, we throw a sop to that persistent call by going on fishing-or-hunting trips—as far away as possible from the haunts of Man. Or we summer in mock-primitiveness at some alleged outpost of civilization. In *Broken Fang*, the reader gains a vicarious thrill and a momentary mental lapse into the primal world by following Bart thither. The excursion satisfies a subtle but strong need.

Perhaps many a frontiersman knows the wolfish mode of life and the strange nature of the wolf-pack as thoroughly as does the creator of *Broken Fang*. But to no writer, in my memory, has it been given to paint that life and that savage and wily nature more convincingly and with more powerfully dramatic strokes.

Far too often a writer of dog-sagas falls into the inexcusable blunder of giving his hero the ratiocinations and impulses of a human. As sanely attribute to a canary a profound knowledge of quadratic equations! Dog-thought and Man-thought are poles apart. Thricewise is the author who can avoid the pitfall of making the two overlap.

Bart is all *dog*. He thinks as a dog. He conducts himself throughout as a dog. His creator has mastered in full the secrets of canine reasoning and complexes. This feat by itself makes his book stand out from the ruck of dog-narratives.

Even more noteworthy is his handling of the mental processes which permit Bart to shed the outward semblance of doghood and revert to the ways of his wolf-ancestors. This is masterly. It is a bit of flawless expert artistry. Ever the reader waits worriedly for the false note which shall smear the whole. Ever he waits in vain.

God—or Nature—or Evolution—set the Dog apart from the Wolf by giving him an innate worship for Man. In Bart's wildest lupine phases, this worship is forever tugging at him. The conflict is splendidly portrayed and without one blot of maudlin sentiment. It convinces. It convinces because it is *true*.

Of all the world, the Dog and Man alone love Man. How or when or whence this strange bond between the two had its beginning, we do not know. Nobody knows—though everybody guesses. Perhaps one guess is as good as another. But the fact remains that every quadruped, save only the Dog, hates Man or is icily indifferent to him or dreads him or serves him dully in return for food and lodging. The Dog alone is voluntarily his chum and serf.

If the Wolf is the sole ancestor of the Dog—as many scientists claim he is—when did the sharp line of demarcation begin and under what conditions? Bring up a wolf-cub as a pet; and soon or late he will revert to type. So it cannot be alone a matter of environment and of early training that makes him Man's foe.

But there are a score of proven instances in which a dog, brought up in the wilderness as a creature of the forests, has been tamed and trained at last by some man; and gladly he has forsaken the cave for the hearth. Ever the tugging bond between him and humanity has been impossible to break. Given half an opportunity, it has asserted its mystic force.

When, as with Bart, a dog's youth has been spent in the service of a man who is his god, and when circumstances drive him back to type, the tug of that bond never ceases wholly to make itself felt. He cannot forget the scent and the touch and the voice of the human from whom he is parted; nor the homely lure of wood-smoke and of cooked food and of a bed that is made of boards instead of sod.

At the first real chance to do so, he sheds his wolfish ways of thought and of action; joyously he comes back to his heritage. Hunters and trappers and cow-men by the hundreds can attest to this.

It was so with Bart. And the telling of his wanderings, and of his return, is epic. I like *Broken Fang*. I like it much.

ALBERT PAYSON TERHUNE

BROKEN FANG

CHAPTER I

Murder in the Farthest Pasture

WHITE moonlight flooded the slopes of Stuben Canyon and flashed back from the tumbling creek that rushed and roared between the steep walls of rock. Early summer had brought soft nights and a faint haze to the high country. Far away toward the ragged rims of Chimney Mountain there was no haze; the cold, thin air hung clear as crystal over never melting banks of snow.

At the head of Stuben Canyon where the rock walls flattened out into a wide meadow fringed with spruce and quaking aspens, lay the Circle Bar Cow Ranch. It was a summer camp used for only two months each year as a regular dwelling place, and for three months additional as a refuge and stopping place for tired and hungry riders of the range. Below the log cabins that served as bunk houses stood high, pole corrals and branding chutes.

Above the summer camp lay a series of meadows forming wide, grass-matted steps upward to the very foot of Chimney Mountain. These meadows furnished summer pasture for the Circle Bar cows and their calves.

On this particular night murder was being done in the farthest pasture north, under the frowning lip of Chimney Rock, the sentinel peak of the mountain. A wolf pack was ravaging one of the herds. They had descended like fanged ghosts upon four white-faced cows and their calves. The cows had faced the onslaught for a brief stand. Then they had charged away to circle, bellowing mournfully in the white light.

The leader of the pack, a great king wolf with a wide, black muzzle and stubby ears, had hamstrung one of the calves and hurled it to the ground. He stood like a broad-chested demon above the bawling calf, his fangs dripping blood, while his four followers raced and slashed in pursuit of the other calves.

Down at the Circle Bar cabins the sound of the struggle and the bawling of the frantic mothers was heard by a silent guardian. Bart, breed dog, willing slave of a breed master, heard the challenge of the pack and leaped to the door of his master's cabin. He growled deep in his throat, and when no one answered from within he whimpered impatiently. Pushing the door with a shaggy and powerful shoulder he tried to get into the cabin, but the catch was fastened securely.

Inside the cabin Sioux Charlie was sleeping with his blanket pulled over his head. After hours of hard riding and a big supper of stew and fried potatoes he had fallen into a sound sleep.

Bart growled again, then whirled and headed out into the moonlight toward Chimney Rock. His powerful legs drove him ahead at great strides and his wide muzzle lifted and fell as he leaped along. Bart was a dog with a taint: his father had been almost wild, a slashing, killing brute who had thrown aside the restraints of domestication to mate with a she-wolf; and Bart had inherited his moods and his frame with its stringy muscles and wide chest. Bart feared no wolf; he had never met one that could stand before his savage rush. Sioux Charlie had trained him for a killer and he knew nothing else.

Through the quaking aspens of the lower meadows he raced, the yelping and bawling above him acting as a guide. Entering the spruce belt he increased his pace and his jaws sagged open eagerly. The moonlight flashed upon him as he crossed into open spaces between the clustering spruce groves, and his reddish-grey coat shone dully. His fangs flashed as he galloped

into the moonlight. On the left side where one fang
should have curved downward like a dagger, it ended
in a ragged stump. Sioux Charlie boasted that this was
Bart's only defect.

In the pasture above, the kill was almost ended. The
four younger wolves had driven their victims into the
timber and on to the next meadow. There two of them
had pulled down their beef under the noses of the frantic white-faced cows. The other two raced on enjoying
the chase, playing with their quarry for a while before
slashing it to the ground. The four were all sons of the
lobo wolf who was their leader. They were young and
not seasoned, which accounted for their slow work.

In the first meadow the lobo had not wasted time.
He was a killer and never played with a victim. His
wanderings had led him into the Chimney Rock country and he had selected the Circle Bar herds for his first
raid. He stood with swaying head over the dead calf.
The moonlight glinted from his black muzzle and his
grey coat of coarse hair. His jaws were parted and sag-
ging in an unpleasant grin.

Bart came through the grass like a red-grey hurri-
cane. Straight across the meadow he charged. Here was
an enemy that must be killed. The lobo looked up and
squared himself; but he did not expect the dog to come
on. No dog had ever offered to give him battle. Twice
packs had trailed him and he had whirled upon them

with his ripping fangs and had killed those in the van who could not retreat. But this dog came on, and the lobo's grinning jaws snapped shut.

Bart was as surprised as the lobo when the king wolf did not turn tail. He was used to running his wolf down. Many a wolf would fight when he overtook him, but this was the first killer that had ever faced him, and stood his ground. Hurling himself through the air he leaped upon the lobo.

The wolf side-stepped and slashed out with his cutting fangs. A red gash appeared on Bart's shoulder as he shot past his adversary. Whirling he leaped again. Again the wolf side-stepped, slashing out viciously but refusing to close with the dog. This time he missed and Bart whirled to face him, furious at being played with. Rumbling deep in his chest he crouched and for a second eyed the lobo.

Face to face they stood, fangs bared, ears flattened, watching each other. The white moonlight showed a striking similarity between them. In one detail they were identical. Each had a broken fang on the left side. The lobo had a shade the better of it in weight, but Bart's legs were heavier and stronger, a heritage from some distant dog ancestor.

Bart feinted a charge and the wolf leaped to one side. As he moved Bart sprang and their bodies crashed together. The wolf reared back, slashing and snarling and Bart closed in. With a dull thump they went down, the dog fighting savagely and silently for a throat-hold while the wolf sought to slash his enemy to ribbons and spring clear of a clinch.

The lobo cut Bart's jowls and ripped his shoulders. He could not stop the grim onslaught. Steadily those iron jaws forced their way into the heavy hair over his jugular vein and settled themselves like a vise.

The wolf plunged and rolled dragging Bart over and over. The fight was a silent one now, a finish battle. With a mighty heave the lobo hurled Bart over him. Bart's neck snapped and the strain almost uncoupled his backbone, but he refused to loosen his grip. Sioux Charlie would have said, had he been watching the battle, that Bart's breed mixture was good, that it contained some bull.

Down in the lower meadow the youngsters had heard the start of the battle and had gathered under the spruce trees to watch. Seeing that the dog was giving battle they trotted over, to stand in silent watchfulness, sure that their leader would finish this strange smelling brother. When Bart was not cut down, as they had seen other dogs go down, they edged closer whimpering or snarling as their feelings prompted them.

Bart paid no attention to the pack. He had but one thought: to hang on till the struggling lobo gave in. The fur over the throat was too thick for his single fang

"You do not kill Bart," he said evenly

to cut through. He had resorted to choking tactics, and they were beginning to tell. The lobo's breath hissed through his teeth and he was struggling wildly and without directed effort. Furiously he attempted to shake loose the strangling jaws at his throat.

Bart was now on top, his feet planted firmly, his savage grip tighter than ever. One of the pack swerved uneasily and leaped in close. His fangs cut at Bart's leg tendons. Bart leaped over his prostrate foe and swung the fast weakening lobo between himself and the young wolf. Another of the pack leaped in, and a second later the whole pack was upon the dog.

Bart gave the lobo a final shake that sent him rolling, and whirled to face the youngsters. One of them he caught broadside. He bowled him over, slashing his shoulder. Leaping at a second he closed with him. The pack were no cowards but they lacked the lobo's leadership and they were inexperienced. For a few minutes they gave battle.

In and out they darted slashing the legs and shoulders of the big dog. Then Bart caught one of them and hurled him to the ground. The pack stayed only long enough to free their brother; then they fled.

While Bart whipped off the pack the lobo had a chance to recover his breath. Staggering to his feet he trotted to the edge of the timber and growled low in his throat. The pack was already in flight with Bart at their heels and at this warning growl they scattered into the timber.

Bart whirled at the sound of the king wolf's throaty warning and charged. The king wolf did not stay to fight. He had no appetite for more of Bart's gripping jaws. Like a shadow he vanished into the night. Bart gave chase but soon discovered that his leg muscles were stiffened by the slashing they had received from the young wolves. Halting he stood on the edge of the timber and listened. He wished Sioux Charlie would come and see what he had done.

Lying down in the grass, he began licking his wounds and rumbling deep in his throat.

Silence came to the high country again. The cows ceased their mournful bellowing and only the night breezes in the spruce disturbed the clear quietness. Bart lay still, licking his wounds and watching the little meadow.

A porcupine edged out of the timber and stood sniffing the blood-tainted air. With jerky steps he waddled into the open and sat beside a clump of willows. He did not worry about enemies; even man who was his worst enemy did not worry him. Nature had made him a stolid fellow, without imagination or fear. Bart did not so much as look at the little animal. He had learned early in his puppy days to leave those spiny creatures alone.

Bart did not know why he lingered at the edge of the meadow. His wounds were not serious and he was not tired. He just lay in the grass and watched the carcass of the calf. Presently a shadow slid from the timber and halted for an instant, then vanished. Bart's ears lifted but he did not move. The shadow had appeared to the windward and had not scented him.

Again the form appeared. This time it stood out clearly in the moonlight. It was a dog coyote who had scented the kill. The coyote stood motionless looking at the carcass in the trampled circle of grass. Something about the smells that came to his twitching nose made him uneasy. There was dog scent along with the wolf smell. The coyote moved his long tail and edged closer to the kill.

Bart rose and growled, at which the coyote stiffened and sprang backward like a flash. With a side glance toward Bart he fled into the blue-black shadows of the spruce.

From far up on the mountain a call rang down the wind. A long drawn, defiant call, the cry of the king wolf before the hunt. Bart stirred at this challenge, then lifted his muzzle to the white moon and answered with a defiant howl. He would meet the challenge of the lobo and when they met again the fight would be to a finish. Waiting a second he swung down the mountain toward the Circle Bar Ranch. He was sure the pack would not kill again that night, and he would be on their trail the next day.

At the foot of Chimney Rock the lobo halted his pack. He had found a country that was not his and would not be his without a struggle, and he liked that country. He was determined to stay and meet the challenge of the breed dog. No wolf or dog had ever dared dispute supremacy with him before, and he refused to be driven off.

Leading his young pack into a rocky hollow that was almost inaccessible he sat down with them. The next time he met that dog he would know how to fight him and he would use the pack to advantage. After the next meeting none would dispute the one who ruled the Chimney Rock range. Lobo liked that range. It was well stocked with fat calves, and was backed by fifty miles of rough country for running on clear nights after a kill, and for mating. The next year would see a bigger pack. Lobo knew it, for he had sighted a trim she-wolf far up in the high country. Soon he would make friends with her and they would run together.

The youngsters were getting restless. They had not gorged as they would have had Bart left them unmolested, and now they were hungry. Lobo got to his feet and shook his massive shoulders. He must give his pups a run and let them pull down a snow-shoe rabbit or two. Out into the moonlight the five headed and slid noiselessly toward the spruce timber below.

Bart came out into the open beside his master's cabin and sat on the flat door-stone watching and listening. He did not want to wake Sioux Charlie but something was bothering him. He had a vague feeling that all was not well, that there was trouble ahead. His memory was not good, but he could not forget how his master had cared for him and trained him. Sioux Charlie was all that Bart considered in the world. He hated wolves, and he disdained bobcats and other lesser wild folk. Now as he sat in the white light he was worried, and his worry seemed to have something to do with Sioux Charlie.

As a pup he had played all over this yard beside the cabin. Sioux Charlie had trained him to know a trap and how it was hidden. Down by the corrals they had spent hours making sets and having Bart uncover them. Sioux Charlie wanted his dog to miss the fate they imposed on wolves: the agony of the steel trap. He had even trained Bart to spring a trap without getting caught in the snapping jaws. That was a stunt he often displayed when he was showing his dog off to the cowboys.

Bart did not know it, but the restless feeling came from his blood. He was not all man-beast; he had a taint of wolf, a color in his blood that was bad. Men of the range noted it and shook their heads. They were afraid the powerful wolf killer might some day go as his father had, back to his own blood. Sioux Charlie was not afraid, he trusted Bart and had faith in the training he had given the dog.

The moon sank behind the rim of Chimney Mountain and darkness settled. Bart got up and stretched, tested the wind, with his black muzzle lifted high, and trotted to the pile of spruce boughs that Charlie had fixed for his bed. He wanted to lift his call to the wind, to send defiance ringing toward the high country, but he was afraid of waking his master. Sioux Charlie always scolded when Bart voiced the wolf cry, and he seldom let himself go to that extent.

Curling up on his spruce bed he closed his eyes and was soon breathing deeply and regularly in sleep.

CHAPTER II

The Broken Fang

SIOUX CHARLIE stood at the door of his cabin in the early morning sun. He flexed his arms above his head and his black eyes scanned the slopes below the cabin. Rounding his lips he gave a shrill whistle. A second later Bart came leaping toward him. The hunter immediately noticed his dog's wound. Kneeling he caught the big fellow around the shoulders.

"You been in fight, beeg one," he said softly. Examining the gash his eyes narrowed. "A beeg wolf, a bad wolf." He muttered. "There will be work for us, beeg fellow."

Bart growled deep in his throat and rubbed his broad muzzle against his master's leg. Pulling away he ran to the corner of the cabin.

"A kill and you would show it. I bet one slab of tobacco it is king wolf this time. You wait. After we eat, then we take Boss Parsons and go see this kill."

Charlie straightened and stepped back into his cabin.

In a short time the air was filled with the smoke of frying bacon and the odor of coffee. Bart watched Charlie hungrily. He was not hungry for food; what he wanted was a look or a pat from the busy hunter, and he got them every time Charlie passed him.

"You let me sleep while you hunted. Have I not told you different?" Charlie pointed a long hunting knife at Bart then thrust it into the frying pan and turned a slice of bacon.

Bart wiggled his rump joyfully and let his heavy jaws sag open in a broad dog-smile. His fears of the night before had vanished and he was happy.

"Breakfast ready?" A deep voice called from the door.

Bart leaped to his feet and grew tense, his jaws closed tight over his white teeth.

Charlie turned from the stove to greet the visitor. "All ready, Boss Parsons," he called. "You eat with Bart and me?"

"I have had breakfast, thanks, but I'll step in for a minute." The owner of the Circle Bar Ranch stepped over the threshold. He kept a watchful eye on the great dog in the center of the floor. He respected Bart but he did not exactly like him. The brute was too savage, too much a one-man dog to be liked.

"It is good you came. Bart has made a kill and I know it is a king wolf, a lobo; maybe the lobo Jerry was fighting all last summer over on Battlement." Charlie beamed confidently.

"The dog looks as though he had been in a fight, all right," Parsons agreed.

"He has made a kill, no? If not he would not be here. When Bart, he meets a wolf and fights, it is a dead wolf." Charlie seated himself at the table and began to eat.

"I hope it is that old wolf Jerry was telling about," Parsons replied. "Jerry said he fought that demon for a year and never even got a shot at him. He's trap wise and poison wise, never eats except from his own kill. And to add insult to injury he raised a pack of whelps right over on Battlement and Jerry never got one of them." Parsons looked at Bart.

"Jerry he has no killer like Bart to run them down with. We get that beeg feller—if he isn't dead like a stone right now." Charlie tossed a piece of bacon rind to Bart.

The big dog rumbled deep in his throat and gulped down the tasty bit of meat.

"Are you sure it's wise to let Bart run loose? He might start killing on his own, or he might even head a pack if you have left any wolves in the Chimney Rock country." Parsons eyed the dog at his feet uncertainly.

"Bart has the training like a dog should. He hates wolves. I have taught him so." Charlie spoke positively.

"But he's part wolf and he's a savage brute." Parsons was still unconvinced. "I'm sure glad I wasn't the victim he broke that fang on," he added as Bart grinned exposing his broken fang.

"Bart has made the kill. We follow him and find it," Charlie said rising and wiping his mouth on the sleeve of his wool shirt. Jamming an old felt hat on his head he slipped into his hunting coat and reached for his rifle.

Bart leaped out through the open door eagerly. He was ready to lead Charlie to the pasture above. The two men followed Bart down to the corner of the corral. Here they saddled their horses and made ready to strike out.

The grass was dripping from the night's heavy dew and the drops of water on the tips of the blades glistened in the sun. Bart shouldered his way through the young growth and sloshed through the grass, stopping every few hundred yards to shake the water from his heavy coat.

A squirrel chattered noisily in the top of a spruce, tossing down dry cones in his excitement and scolding as fast as he could. From behind a fallen log leaped a snow-shoe rabbit; his wide-set eyes rolled in terror as Bart swung past him. But the great dog did not give him a second glance. High up near the foot of Chimney Rock, Bart slowed his pace and cut through the timber with a watchful swinging of his head. Twice he paused to test a cross trail with its scent marker in the form of a moss covered boulder or a whitened skull. He could read the signs of the passing travelers from those cross trail sign posts. No member of the wolf family, be he coyote or timber wolf would pass a sign post without leaving his scent. Bart hoped he would find fresh sign of the lobo and his pack, an indication that they had come down from the high country again that night or early in the morning.

Charlie noticed the actions of his dog and pushed forward hitching his rifle to a ready position on the saddle horn. Parsons spurred up beside him and jogged silently along. He was wondering what they would find.

Bart burst out into the meadow where he had fought the lobo and leaped across the open grass to where the slain calf lay. Two black and white magpies soared upward, and sailed down into the timber. At this sure sign of death Charlie and Parsons urged their horses to a gallop. Pulling up beside the carcass they halted. Charlie got down slowly, a disappointed look on his face.

"It is the work of a wolf and his pack," he said straightening after examining the carcass and the tracks around it. "There has been a fight as I said."

Parsons did not reply, but slid from his horse and stood over his calf. After a brief but searching look he knelt and examined its hamstrung tendons. His eyes darkened and he got to his feet.

"I'm afraid you have been wrong, Charlie," he said, not unkindly. Pointing to the calf's rump he went on. "Those gashes were made by a killer with only one tearing fang." He looked at Bart and loosened his six gun at his hip. "I mean Bart," he finished evenly.

Bart was running around in circles sniffing the tracks of the pack, searching eagerly for signs to show that the wolves had returned. He did not pay any attention to the two men who stood facing each other tensely.

Charlie fell on his knees and examined the gashes in the flesh, then he examined the tracks in the trampled grass. Shaking his head he faced Parsons. "No, Boss Parsons, it is the wolf, lobo, from the Battlement come to this range."

"This is serious, Charlie. Beef is valuable nowadays. We can't afford to lose many critters. There was a pack, I can see that, but the marks on this calf have settled the thing for me. Bart is heading that pack." Parsons balanced his gun as he spoke. He was quick-tempered and stubborn and just now he was convinced

that the big dog circling about at the edge of the
timber was a beef killer. He had seen wolf dogs go
bad before.

Charlie stepped in front of his boss. "You do not
kill Bart," he said evenly without raising his voice,
his black eyes looking squarely into those of his boss.

Parsons lowered his gun and a grin came to his lips.
This boy would fight for his dog. Cross breeds of the
wilderness, both of them, but each dead loyal to the
other. At any rate Parsons was convinced that Charlie
was loyal to the coarse haired brute he had raised. The
look in the breed's eyes said plainly that he would kill
to save his dog or to avenge him.

"I'll give you a couple of days to bring in that lobo,
and then if this killing continues, Bart goes." Parsons
put up his gun with a snap. "I'll have the boys keep an
eye out for wolves—and for dogs." Finishing he swung
into his saddle.

Bart saw the men mounting their horses and he
leaped away to lead them to the meadows just below
where the young wolves had made their kill. Parsons
spurred ahead close to Bart's heels.

As they came to the second carcass Parsons got to the
ground, his face dark. Glancing down the slope he saw
the third carcass.

"This will have to be cleared up now. Another kill
like this one will stand us to lose two hundred dollars.

Beef is not dirt cheap now—like it used to be." He glared at Bart. "Tie up that brute tonight and tie him tight."

Charlie's face never changed as he nodded. Its blank, wind tanned features were a mask; but underneath that mask he was worrying. Jerry, the Battlement hunter, had fought the lobo all one year and had failed to get him. He was being given two days to pull down the brute. His eyes wandered to where Bart was growling and sniffing at a blood clot in the grass and they lighted a little. He had Bart, and Bart had already met the wolf. Today he would take his dog and strike for the high country.

Parsons kicked the stiff carcass with his foot. "Not worth skinning," he snapped.

"I go now to take up the trail," Charlie said simply.

Parsons nodded gloomily, "I wish you'd get rid of that dog. I still think he's the killer."

Charlie shrugged his shoulders. "It is the lobo," he said with irritating evenness.

Parsons stood and watched Charlie mount and ride away with Bart leading out eagerly ahead. Swinging into his own saddle he headed back toward the camp.

On the way down to the cabins he thought and planned. He could not afford to humor Charlie to the extent of losing three or four calves every night. Precautionary measures must be taken. He had formed a

plan by the time he reached the camp. His range foreman, Tex Lee, was leaning against the horse corral,
smoking.

"Mornin' boss," drawled Tex.

Parsons nodded curtly and Tex straightened. Here
was trouble. When the boss acted that way something
was wrong.

"Three calves are down in the meadows—wolves—
or dogs. Possibly a wolf pack headed by a dog. One of
the calves was ripped open by a brute with a broken
fang," Parsons said deliberately.

"Sioux Charlie's killer gone back to his own?" Tex
asked the question more as though he were making a
statement.

"Charlie says not. He says it was the work of the
pack from the Battlement headed by a big lobo, but
I'm not convinced." Parsons got down and turned his
horse loose.

"I wouldn't trust that dog. He looks bad and he's a
killer by nature." Tex snapped the head off a mountain
daisy with his quirt as he spoke.

"I want you to have the boys scatter out for the next
few days and ride all of the range they can cover, and I
want them to watch for kills and for evidence. They
may shoot to kill if they are sure that the dog is killing,
or if he is heading a pack. And that dog is to be tied up
tonight at sundown. If he's running tonight, shoot him."

Parsons turned on his heel and headed for the cabin he used as his own.

Tex strode down to the lower corrals where his men were waiting for their orders. His lips were set tight and he was wondering what the outcome of his orders would be.

Up on the slopes above Bart and Charlie were pushing along at a smart pace. Charlie realized that he had a big job ahead of him, and he did not intend to waste any time getting to it.

By ten o'clock they had picked up the trail of the pack where the youngsters had chased rabbits and played among the rocks at the foot of Chimney Rock. Bart took up the trail eagerly and followed it with a long stride that soon outdistanced the horse Charlie was riding.

The trail wound in and out along the base of the cliffs that towered upward a sheer thousand feet to form the landmark that was known as Chimney Rock. The pack had been playing as they passed along; there was plenty of evidence of that. Bart could see where one of the youngsters had chased a porcupine to a flat stone where the spiny little bark-gnawer had shoved his snout under cover and had dared the wolf to do his worst. All around the flat stone, but at a safe distance, were jaw marks to show that the young wolf had made a great fuss. But he had been too wise to attack.

The report of the rifle shattered the silence

Then there was a jumble of tracks and a padded space under a spreading balsam where the pack had gathered around Lobo for a consultation. Possibly they had treed a wild cat; the bark of the balsam smelled of cat.

From the base of the cliff the trail straightened and headed toward the breaks and ridges that sloped away from the square-shouldered peak. Bart knew that fifty miles of rough going spread at his feet, but the trail was fairly hot and he had Charlie at his back. Somehow he wanted to meet Lobo and make his kill that day. A warning sense urged him on. But if he outdistanced his master, Charlie would return to the cabin and he might not find him there when he returned in the morning.

Charlie urged his horse on, keeping to the general direction Bart had taken. He was eager to keep up. But most he wanted Bart to overtake the wolf so he did not call him back. He must take some chances because of the short time in which they had to work. Reaching the edge of the rough country Charlie paused. The pack and Bart had headed down into the wildest stretch of the mountain.

Pushing on, he let his horse lag to a fast walk. He knew now that the trail was going to be a long one and that he could not push his cayuse too hard.

Noon came and Bart was still out ahead. The only

living thing Charlie had seen was a camp robber.
Nature has made the camp robber the friendliest of all
the wilderness birds. This particular fellow cocked his
dark head and looked at Charlie hungrily. Charlie
tossed him a crumb of cold biscuit from his lunch and
the trim beggar hopped almost up to the hunter's boot
to get it.

Charlie munched his food, and watched the black
and white camp robber clean up the crumbs. Bart was
far away in the breaks by now. The man knew the
great dog would not slacken his pace until he came to
the end of the trail or until hunger drove him back to
the cabin. Bart would not kill for food; he had been
trained that way. Charlie could not help worrying as
he remembered Parson's orders to have the dog tied
up that night. Bart might run till morning. Even if he
himself did not stay out he would wait up for the dog,
and see that he arrived safely in camp.

That afternoon the hunter pushed on as far as he
dared into the broken country. Then he turned back
toward the head of Stuben Canyon. He had not sighted
the pack or Bart, but he had seen signs that encouraged
him. Bart would have to shift for himself if he met
the wolves this day.

It was ten o'clock when Charlie turned his cayuse
loose to graze and entered his cabin. He knew that only
a few of the boys were in because the saddle pegs of

several were bare. This did not disturb him, for cowboys ride late and often sleep out wherever night overtakes them. The moonlight would make riding easy and safe.

The lights were out in all the cabins. Charlie entered his own without waking anyone. Building a fire he prepared supper for himself. After supper he wound and set a battered old alarm clock. The time he set on the luminous dial was four o'clock.

CHAPTER III

The She-Wolf's Choice

ALL day Bart ran through the thin air. He had never
followed a wolf pack that covered so much ground
and kept up such a pace. Lobo was indeed a fellow to be
reckoned with. Toward evening Bart could tell that
the leader had been forcing his whelps to run. At one
spot there had been an argument and the leader had
hurled the balky member to the ground and had stood
over him. After that the trail straightened out again.
It was plain that Lobo was a hard master.

Dusk came and Bart halted at a clear stream to drink.
After lapping his fill of the cold mountain water he
took up the trail again. The moon came up and a sharp
coldness close to frost settled over the whitening land-

scape. Bart sighted a doe sliding from brush clump to brush clump, eternally on the alert for enemies. He gave the doe only a glance but when she sighted him she bounded away in fright.

The trail was really getting hot now and Bart was pushing forward at a distance-devouring pace, filling his broad chest with cold air and letting his tongue loll out as he ran.

Swinging out on a knoll he saw that the trail forked. Lobo had cut off to the right while the youngsters had circled to the left. Bart halted and sniffed. He could overtake the pack easily, their trail scattered as soon as their leader left them. It was different with the trail of Lobo. It cut straight down the slope. Bart flattened his ears and shot away on the king wolf's scent.

Running evenly, but at top speed he crossed a ridge and hit a sage flat. In the center of the flat he sighted two wolves. One was a slender she-wolf with a trim muzzle and a beautiful bushy tail. Something inside Bart swelled up against his ribs and he slowed to a walk. An urge was pounding within him that he had never known before. Here was a trim mate and at her side stood his enemy, Lobo. Bart approached slowly, undecided what to do. The mating call was surging up in him, the call his father had answered before him. And to confuse him more, there stood his enemy. Bart growled deep and lunged forward.

Lobo saw the dog and whirled to face him. No male had ever dared challenge his selection of a mate; but this dog was different. His was a violence that Lobo sensed would not be stopped until one or the other lay stretched in the sage. Sending a warning call to the pack that he knew was rabbit-hunting close by, he set himself for the expected charge.

The slender she-wolf whimpered and slipped away to a safe distance. Turning she watched the two contenders for her favor.

Bart hurled himself upon the wolf, forgetting in his fury and excitement over the she-wolf all he had learned the night before. Lobo leaped aside and slashed out viciously. Bart twisted in the air and lost his balance. He missed the ripping fangs but fell heavily, rolling over in the sage. Lobo saw his advantage and sprang. Ripping and slashing he descended upon the dog.

The strain of bull in Bart worked instinctively. Flat on his back he reached up and his great jaws crushed down on Lobo's shoulder. They sank in with a sickening crunch. The king wolf reared back and shook himself to rid his shoulder of the searing pain that shot through it, then he savagely attacked Bart's head and ears.

The pack heard Lobo's warning and came leaping over the sage to watch the fight. They circled about the struggling battlers watching narrowly. One of them edged over to the she-wolf's side and muzzled up close

to her. She snapped at him and backed off. Her heart
was with the two big fellows at death grips below.

Bart stood the slashing fangs as long as he could.
Now he loosened his hold and hurled the wolf from
him. Like a flash they charged again. Forgotten was all
the cunning each knew. Only the feel for the other's
throat was in each brain. They crashed together and fell
heavily, each seeking for the death grip at the other's
throat.

Three of the pack had closed in. The fourth was
beginning to assert himself with the she-wolf. He
shouldered her toward the knoll above, ripping her
viciously on the flanks. With a longing look back at the
two fighters she whirled and trotted away. The youngster who had dominated her was a big fellow. It was
he who had been trounced by Lobo for lagging that
afternoon.

Lobo saw the she-wolf leave and recognized a rival
within his pack. Shaking himself free he leaped aside
and charged up the hill. Bart sprang after him to meet
the bared fangs of the three youngsters. With a bellow
he leaped upon the nearest wolf and crushed him to the
ground. The other two closed in grimly, eager for
battle.

Bart hurled them from him and shook the unlucky
whelp he had closed with. The youngster fought
gamely but a grip on his throat quieted him. Bart did

not wait to choke the life out of him but hurled him aside and leaped at one of the others. By this time Lobo and the she-wolf had disappeared. From beyond the knoll floated the yelps of the ambitious pup.

The three youngsters leaped back from Bart. Here was a real leader and they suddenly wanted to convince him they had only been playing. Bart was almost winded and stood breathing heavily, snarling defiance but unable to get his jaws upon any of the pack.

Remembering the she-wolf he turned and started up the little hill. The three youngsters dropped in behind eager to follow this new leader. Bart whirled and charged them. They scattered and he returned to the trail of Lobo. The three dropped in behind again. Bart let them follow and struck out after his rival. He had only one thought and that was to get his fangs into the king wolf again.

A horse and rider had paused at the top of the knoll. Tex Lee had ridden far that day and was returning late. Hearing the struggle at the foot of the knoll he had cut down that way to see what was going on. As he sat watching the moonlit slope of silver sage Bart swung into view with the trailing wolves at his heels. He was running madly, his head down and his ears back and the youngsters were leaping along behind.

Tex loosened his rifle from the saddle and swung it upward. The light was uncertain but he would chance a shot. Parsons had been right: Charlie's dog was running at the head of a pack. Tex took quick aim and fired.

As the report of the rifle shattered the silence the three wolves broke and fled in different directions. Bart never missed a stride. He glanced up at the rider who was now trying to quiet his horse. A bullet tore away a sage root at his heels but he did not slow his pace. When he had finished the king wolf he would stop. He knew the man was not Sioux Charlie and he never paid any attention to any other human being.

Tex tried to follow the dog but soon lost him in the shadows of a grove of spruce. Turning his horse toward home he rode away. The dog would come in the next day and they could finish him. There was no doubt now as to his guilt.

Bart ran swiftly, his strength returning as he followed the trail of the two he sought. After a half mile of going he overtook the young wolf who had tried to make up with the she-wolf. The whelp turned tail and fled up the mountain. Bart let him go and ran on. A few minutes later he sighted Lobo and the slim grey mate running swiftly side by side.

The three wolves who had been scattered by the shot had taken up the trail of their newly elected leader and were yelping eagerly as they followed. Bart snarled deep in his throat and leaped forward. The big king wolf heard Bart and shouldered his slim companion in a short circle. Bart swung across to meet his rival.

The dog and the wolf faced each other in the white moonlight, each watching with blazing eyes and parted jaws for an opening. The three youngsters swung into sight and circled around the tense, grey forms of the rivals. Softly the she-wolf slipped away to the shadows of the spruce to wait the outcome. Lobo swung his head from side to side. He was furious at his pack for deserting him and could not decide whether to hurl himself upon the whelps or to finish Bart.

Bart was watching the grey form in the shadows out of the tail of his eye. Forgotten was his hatred of all wolves. Here was one he would make an exception of. Lobo stirred and edged toward one of his sons. He wanted the pack with him. The youngster whimpered and looked uncertain. Lobo lunged at him savagely. The young wolf broke and fled with Lobo at his heels. For a second Bart doubled himself for a spring, then he waited.

It did not matter to him whether the king wolf whipped his pack into line or not. He did not want them. And given time he would run each young wolf down and finish him.

Lobo drove his sons into the timber and backed them up against a bank. Eagerly they accepted him, the runt of the pack rolling on his back in supplication. Having

made sure of his support, Lobo whirled to give battle
to Bart but the dog was gone and with him the slim
grey mate he had picked to run with. Lobo sent his
challenge down the wind and gave chase.

Bart had intended to attack Lobo, but the new and
queer feeling within him mastered his wrath and he ran
to the shadows where she stood. Shouldering up to her
he waved his thick tail and lifted his ears in true dog
fashion.

The slim wolf showed her fangs and edged
away. Bart snapped at her shoulder and growled
angrily. The she-wolf whimpered and leaned toward
him. Bart ran a step or two and looked back. The slim
wolf was at his shoulder. With a throaty cry he headed
out into the moonlight.

Racing madly the two headed down across the slope
toward the head of Stuben Canyon. The slim shadow
at the great dog's side proved to be swift and light of
foot. Eagerly she raced and leaped as they cleared
fallen logs and low bushes. On and on mile after mile
they ran. At their backs the king wolf and his pack gave
up the chase and spread out to hunt.

Bart led his mate to a rocky ridge overlooking the
summer camp of the Circle Bar Ranch. Here he halted
and they sat looking down over the moon-flooded
valley. The slim wolf edged close to Bart's side and
they watched while deep shadows crept up the side of

Stuben Canyon and slowly spread a blanket of darkness over the meadows at the head of the canyon.

As daylight approached Bart began coaxing his mate to follow him down to the cabins, but she would only go as far as the rim overlooking the valley. She had been taught to avoid the habitations of man. After several fruitless attempts Bart came back to her and sat down.

She moved restlessly up the hill trying to get him to follow. At last Bart gave in and trotted after her up the mountain.

The she-wolf ran perhaps a mile then cut up a steep rock strewn side hill. At the foot of a towering Engelmann spruce they came to a cave. The slim grey wolf entered the cave and Bart followed. Stretching herself on the floor she closed her eyes and went to sleep. Bart stood for a long time looking down at her then walked out of the cave. He understood what she wanted. He was to go on down. She would be waiting for him when he returned.

Bart loped down the mountain toward the camp with a light swing. He was happy, but he was worried. Somehow the presence of the grey mate in the cave above seemed to change him. He was not approaching the home ranch as eagerly as he always had before.

The men were lounging at the corrals when Bart came into the clearing. Tex Lee had just told of seeing

Bart running with three young wolves and of how he had missed a moonlight shot. Sioux Charlie had sat silent through the recital, his face a blank, his fingers playing with the stock of his rifle.

"There he comes now," Tex shouted leaping to his feet and whipping out his revolver.

Sioux Charlie shifted his rifle to his knees. "Yes, he come and I 'tend to him. Sit down!" The breed's voice was soft but it was cold and even.

"You're going to shoot him, aren't you?" Tex demanded. He spoke sharply but he sat down.

"Yes, we're going to shoot him, and do it now." Parsons spoke deliberately.

Sioux Charlie got to his feet and whistled to Bart. The big dog leaped toward his master and growled joyfully. Charlie let Bart fawn on him and rubbed his head.

Without a look at the men seated beside the corral he led Bart toward his cabin.

Parsons got to his feet and followed Charlie. He was determined to have it out with the hunter. At the door of the other's cabin he paused to look in.

Bart was sitting in the middle of the floor and Charlie was leaning against the table looking down at him.

"You been bad, feller. Now for not getting that king wolf, Lobo, and for keeping bad company I kill you like the boss say, but they don't shoot you down like a thief—I 'tend to that like the big chief you be." Charlie's mouth twitched and he glared at Bart. "I know, feller, that you have no made the kill."

Outside the door Parsons drew back. Here was real drama. The breed was treating his dog as he would have treated a brother who had betrayed him. Softly he left the cabin, unwilling to eavesdrop on anything so intimate as this meeting. Never before had he seen emotion on the face of his hunter.

Inside the cabin Charlie was watching Bart. The big dog knew that all was not well, and edged over to rest his massive head on the hunter's knee.

"It might be that you are good," Charlie mused. "But it does not look like it."

Bart whimpered a little and moved his head up and down.

"You have been fighting and let that Lobo get away again," Charlie said impatiently. "He must be a wolf of wolves to stand up to you. It is like Jerry says, this Lobo is a bad one."

Bart shook himself and yawned; he was tired and sleepy.

"You do not sleep, feller," the breed muttered softly. "You sleep tonight in the hunting grounds where we had to send your father. Get up and come." Charlie snapped his fingers.

Bart got to his feet obediently and followed Charlie outside. Though dragged out with his efforts of the night he was willing to do anything Charlie asked. The hunter shouldered his rifle and headed toward the rim above the camp.

CHAPTER IV

The Death Sentence

SIOUX CHARLIE walked along with a grim and resolute set to his shoulders. Bart trotted ahead without his usual capers, he was tired and not enthusiastic about setting out again. His hard run of the night before, he felt, should have earned him a sleep through the heat of the day.

Up into the timber they climbed toward the rim where Bart and the she-wolf had sat in the moonlight. Charlie was determined to give Bart a fitting finish and one that he himself would have liked. He had in mind the stony backbone of rock that overlooked the valley. That would make a proper resting place for the bones of the killer who had ranged the valleys of the Chimney Mountain country.

"Beeg Feller!" was all he said

Charlie paused on a jutting point and looked down over the sweeping country. Through the clear, thin air he could see miles of range and on into the impenetrable breaks and sage mesas of the wilderness beyond the tall grass slopes of Chimney Rock range. Landmarks fifty miles away looked close in that land of clear air. The mountains rose silent and moody, their bare shoulders jutting upward above the timber line. This was his country, the land of his people, although they were now moved southward into the barren desert reservations the white man had forced upon them.

Bart stirred and sniffed at the trail he and the slim grey wolf had made that morning. He wanted to lead Charlie to her cave, to show his master what he had found, but something made him hesitate. Possibly it was the way the grey one had acted when he tried to coax her to follow him to the camp.

Charlie paid no attention to the big dog. He was looking back upon other days when he had camped in the valley below with his mother. Charlie could not remember his father, though he knew there had been a stocky trapper who had lived with the Indians and who had made a four hundred mile trip out to the nearest town to marry his mother. The father had been lost in a summer blizzard, early for even that high country—one of those unheralded storms that descend from the snow line and bury the green slopes below.

There was a touch of sadness in the Indian's heart. He had loved his dog and had spent long hours training him. They had been companions for the past two years. Charlie had a rigid sense of honor and loyalty, but above it all he held to the laws of the range. A killer must be put out of the way and Bart, it seemed, had turned killer. Charlie knew Parsons and Tex Lee would not lie, that they were honest in believing Bart guilty. In spite of all their evidence Charlie, himself, was not convinced.

Bart had wandered on up the ridge and Charlie whistled to him. The dog trotted into view wagging his tail. He gave a short deep bark and turned upward again. It was plain that he wanted his master to follow.

Charlie broke his reverie and began to climb again. He would follow Bart. One spot would do as well as another.

Running along eagerly now, Bart headed upward. He was on the trail to the hiding place of the she-wolf. The dim fear he had felt was overcome by his eagerness to see his slim mate. He did not consider what the hunter would do when he saw the wolf because he did not know that a she-wolf is always marked for death in a cow country, that her pelt is worth more than that of a half dozen dog-wolves because she rears a litter of pups each summer.

Charlie took up the trail with a spark of interest as he noted the change in Bart. The dog had something to show him and he would see it before he carried out the thing he had set his mind upon.

They topped the ridge and struck out upon a bench that led to another ridge rising steeper and rockier, its spruce and balsam wind-bent and twisted from fighting the gales that swept the higher reaches.

Half-way across the bench Bart yelped fiercely and leaped ahead; he had sighted something that sent him into an instant rage. Charlie whistled shrilly and shouted. Bart halted in his tracks obedient to his long training. Looking over the sweep of open meadow Charlie saw a big wolf and four grown pups loping away toward the cover of the spruce above.

"Lobo and his pack," he muttered softly. For a moment he was ready to send Bart after them, then he choked back the order to run. If Bart was in with that pack he would be gone for the rest of the day and that night. Trotting to his dog's side he caught Bart by the scruff of the neck.

Bart strained forward, his eyes blazing and his teeth bared. Charlie watched him narrowly. A queer light began to flicker in the depths of the hunter's black eyes. Bart was not acting like a friend to these wolves; he was raging mad.

"What a brute," he muttered shifting his gaze to

the loping king wolf who was out of range of his rifle by this time. "No wonder Jerry could not beat him." Then he looked back to Bart. "But you are his match and I know it, feller," he addressed the dog.

Bart struggled to free himself. He knew that Lobo was on the trail of the slim grey one in the cave above and he wanted to hurl himself at the king wolf's throat.

"Not today, feller; anyway not for a while. We think," Charlie said firmly. "Back!" he snapped.

Bart pulled loose and settled into a slow trot—not after the king wolf, but up toward the broken rim above. He could not understand why he was restrained from attacking his enemy, but he was, and so he would lead Charlie straight to the cave. That would keep the pack from finding the grey one.

Charlie was thinking hard and did not pay attention to the direction Bart had taken. His mind was in a turmoil of uncertainty, though his wind-tanned face showed no trace of his feelings. The actions of his dog convinced him that Bart was no member of the pack, nor had he run with them. Something was wrong here, and he knew it, but could not find a solution.

Reaching the rocky side of the rim Bart broke into a run and Charlie had to call him back several times to keep from losing him. The big fellow leaped and growled impatiently, his teeth flashing in a wide dog smile. He was nearing the cave and eager to show Charlie what he had there.

At the mouth of the cave Bart halted and looked back. His master was toiling upward slowly. In fact Charlie was fighting a stubborn fight with himself. He was trying to decide what to do with the big brute who waited so eagerly for him on the ledge above.

Charlie climbed to the mouth of the cave and halted. He was still in doubt. Bart growled deep in his throat and stepped into the cool shadows of the cave. Charlie slipped his rifle from its strap on his shoulder and looked at the safety. Pushing Bart forward with a slap on the back he stepped into the cave.

The cave was low and he had to stoop to avoid butting his head on its jagged ceiling. The light was poor, too, and he stepped forward slowly so as to allow his eyes to accustom themselves to the gloom. His rifle was ready for instant use, its hammer back against the upper grip plate.

The cave was deep and wide for a few yards, then it pinched down. Bart halted in the open room and stood rigid. He was surprised and disappointed. The room was empty! Sniffing about he located the spot where the grey mate had lain. Walking around the room he tested the air. The place smelled of her strongly; she had been there only a little while before.

Charlie looked about the cave and his lips parted in

a smile. Bart had offered a settlement of the problem. Here was a cave where he could hide his dog until he was sure of himself, until he had time to find out a few things he wanted to know. He had brought a collar and chain with him; it was to have served a part in that final ceremony he had planned. Pulling the collar and chain from his pack sack he slipped the leather band about Bart's neck.

Bart growled and tugged to get free. He wanted to search the cave more thoroughly, to make sure the slim mate had really gone. He did not want a collar around his neck. He had not been chained with that collar since he was an overgrown pup and given to chasing calves, and the strap was uncomfortably tight and narrow. He was not sure the grey one had left. How could he be when he had not looked in every dark corner? Then there was the lobo; she might have left the cave and now, perhaps, was where the big wolf could find her. What would the pack do to a she-wolf who had mated with a dog?

Charlie looked about the cave and discovered a solid slab of rock jutting from the wall. Pulling out his hunting knife he began grooving the pillar so that the chain would not slip from it. The sand rock shaved away under the blade of the knife and in a few minutes Charlie had Bart solidly chained to the wall of the cave.

"You stay here till tomorrow morning. Then I come, and bring food and water. Be a good feller," Charlie said stepping back.

Bart answered with a howl. He did not want to be left chained in that cave. He had work to do and a lot of it. But Sioux Charlie only turned away and left the cave with a noiseless step. He was eager to get started on the plan he had formed for solving the whole knotty problem and saving his dog.

Bart tugged at the chain but it held fast. Hurling his weight upon it, he growled and strained his great head this way and that. The strap around his neck shut off his wind and he had to settle back. As soon as he recovered from one attempt he lunged again and again, but the strap held.

An hour passed and now Bart stretched himself upon the cave floor to wait. Here he must remain prisoner till Charlie came back, and he would endure it in sullen silence.

At the back of the cave something stirred and Bart leaped to his feet. A second later he hurled himself again at the chain. A slender form edged forward out of the gloom. Bart rumbled joyously and hit the end of the chain like a pile driver. The leather around his neck bit deep into his throat, then parted. He was free!

Leaping toward the grey shadow he yelped loudly.

The slim grey one had been in the cave and had heard them approaching. In a panic she had fled into the deepest crack and had lain there trembling while Charlie fastened Bart to the wall.

The man smells and the terrifying chain, now coiled limp on the stone floor, were driving her wild with fear. She huddled close to Bart and would have leaped back into the crevice she had just left but the big dog shouldered her out into the dim light. He could not understand her fear but he knew she was afraid.

She whimpered and showed her white teeth, but she let Bart edge her toward the entrance of the cave. Out in the sunlight they stood a long time watching the mesas below for moving objects. Bart was beginning to wonder if he dared take his slim mate with him to the ranch in the valley.

The grey one settled it for him. She slid noiselessly down among the piled boulders and headed away from the valley straight toward the wilderness across the head of Stuben Canyon. Bart dropped in at her side eagerly. He forgot everything except that she was running at his shoulder.

The run they made was not a carefree rush that answered a surging call for action. The grey one was striking for the distant and inaccessible reaches where she had played as a puppy, and where she knew they would find no man smells and chains. She wanted to take the great dog with her; and with the sure knowledge of her sex she knew he would follow.

Down into Stuben Canyon she led him and along a wall—a trail that would have baffled even a veteran hunter. In the cool shadows at the bottom of the canyon they trotted downward along a rushing stream. Tall fern-like growth brushed their shoulders and scarlet trumpet flowers nodded to them. From rocky crannies the delicate blue of the Colorado columbine stood out against the shadows. Bart breathed deeply and swung along at the side of his chosen mate.

The big dog was catching some of the wariness of the slender she-wolf. A white faced cow snorted from across the stream and he swerved like a shadow to slide beside her into the cover of a clump of willows. There was something about the canyon and the sky above that made Bart's broad chest rise and fall with more than just his deep breathing. He was free for that day at least.

They wound up out of the canyon along a rim that broke off suddenly leaving them in the blue shadows of a timbered hillside. The quaking aspens in the canyon below spread their lighter green against the sombre rock walls and stood out like plumes beside the towering Engelmann spruce whose tops seemed to be striving to peer out over the chasm.

Bart halted and looked back. The she-wolf whimpered and ran on a few steps. Bart seemed loath

to strike out into this new country leaving behind him
Charlie and the ranch. In reality what he felt was the
surge of domestication struggling against the cry of the
wild places and the freedom of the breaks beyond
Chimney Mountain, the same gripping lure that had
taken his father away from the call of duty and the
man made tasks of civilization.

Bart turned and took a step back down the trail he
had just climbed. The grey one darted back and planted
herself in front of him, her slender fangs bared and her
eyes ablaze.

Bart rumbled in his throat and crowded close to her
but she held her ground. Snapping her teeth in his face
she whirled and leaped aside. Bart took a step downward glancing over his shoulder as he did so. The
grey one had not moved. For a long second they stood
that way; then the she-wolf seemed to make up her
mind and leaped away, heading straight for the wilderness.

As she slipped from sight like a silent ghost, Bart
whirled and leaped after her. The call of nature had
won. Leaping madly across the slope he overtook her.
She had slowed her pace when she reached cover and
had lagged hopefully. Seeing that her mate was following she voiced a low cry and darted off.

Across sage flats and through rocky slides, up almost
to the snow line, then back into the valleys they ran,

tirelessly, effortlessly, like machines. Rabbits leaped away from their path in terror but the slender grey one was not hungry. She feared some force would call the powerful mate from her side, and she wanted to carry him deep into the fastness of the unsettled high country.

The long shadows of evening had begun to fill the ravines and canyons with dusk before the grey one slackened her pace. On a ridge just below timber line she halted and seated herself. She was back in her own country where the air held no taint save that of balsam and spruce, a range devoid of cattle, but running over with small game. Within the deep shadows of the lower forests was cover in which to train a pack of squirming puppies, and the grey one was in a home-making mood.

Bart lay down, stretching himself out in perfect relaxation. He was happy and tired and sleepy. The slender mate at his side bent over and licked his nose Bart rumbled deep in his throat and closed his eyes.

CHAPTER V

Wild Blood

SIOUX CHARLIE made a wide circle of the valley and returned to camp from above He had examined cross trails and runs that might be used by the lobo and his pack in coming down from the fastness of the high country. He knew that trap sets would have to be left for months until the travelers on those dim trails lost their wariness. He would set the traps and then resort to poison baits which would serve immediately.

In the yard of his cabin he met Parsons. The boss looked into the stolid face of his hunter and tried to read it. He hated to ask outright if Charlie had killed the dog, but he wanted to make sure. When Charlie said nothing he spoke.

"Did you take care of him?"

"He will not trouble you, Boss Parsons," Charlie said softly.

Parsons nodded sympathetically and turned on his heel.

Charlie entered the cabin and began preparing a meal of bacon and biscuits. His actions were automatic, he was thinking deeply. While the biscuits were baking he prepared some food for his prisoner and filled a canteen with water. These provisions he tucked into his pack-sack along with a tin basin.

Supper was hurried through and Charlie swung his rifle across his back and strapped on his pack-sack. Slipping noiselessly from his cabin he struck out across the clearing toward the rim that overlooked the valley.

He hiked swiftly and in a direct line toward the cave on the upper ridge. The moon came up and made for him a silver path which was splashed with shadow. Charlie trudged on without stopping.

On the first rim he paused and looked down across the range. Far away toward the breaks he could hear a yelping coyote. A minute later the call was answered by a mournful cry from down in the canyon. Charlie started on, then halted again. Another cry floated across to him, the cry of a pack of wolves on the hunt. Lobo was descending with his sons to ravage the pastures of the Circle Bar Ranch.

Charlie looked up at the rim above indecisively.

Should he go on or should he turn back and try to head off the descending killers? He decided that he would be several hours too late to do any good if he did turn back, so he faced toward the cave and began climbing.

At the mouth of the cave he whistled shrilly. No answering bark floated out to him. Swiftly he entered and halted in the thick darkness. Lighting a match he held it high. The flare from his feeble torch glinted back from the chain on the floor. Charlie grunted and stepped forward. Bending he lighted another match and examined the leather collar.

"Beeg feller!" was all he said as he straightened up.

Hurrying out of the cave he stood looking and listening. He wondered if he had been wrong, if Bart was running at the head of that pack that was descending upon the calves in the open meadows at the foot of Chimney Rock. His knowledge of wolves told him that Bart would have to subdue Lobo before he could run at the head of the pack. But Lobo might be getting on in years and have given in to the great dog.

Charlie struck out for the valley. When he examined the kill he would know whether Bart was with the pack. He felt sure of that.

On the way down to the ranch cabins Charlie turned the situation over in his mind. One thing stuck and would not be cleared up. Why had Bart not returned to the cabin? This question kept pounding away in his mind until by the time he reached the cabin he was again willing to believe that Bart had gone wrong. The kill, if it was made, would tell the story.

That night while the boys of the Circle Bar slept, five grey shadows descended from the high country bringing death. At the head ran Lobo, the king wolf; with the cunning of years of ravishing, he led his sons away to the west, far from the breaks. In a little meadow that was fringed with tall grass and that cupped a tiny lake, the pack fell upon a herd of white-faced cows and their calves.

Out of the denser growth, like demons, the young ones leaped on the calves. Slashing and yelping they tore down five of the helpless sucklings while the cows raged and bellowed helplessly. It was a red night for the pack; they gorged themselves with veal and lolled in the tall grass.

Lobo had made his kill at once, hamstringing the bawling calf he had selected and ripping it open without wasting time or energy. He ate his fill then stood watching his sons gorge themselves. No one disturbed them, for Lobo had planned his kill far from the ranch buildings, and the only boys out that night were riding up close to the breaks expecting an attack from that quarter.

Parsons had known that riding at night would not do any good, but he was angry and wanted to prevent

further slaughter. The range to be covered was ten
miles long and eight wide with a fringe of five or six
miles more up canyons and arroyos where the cattle
would feed. Tex Lee had suggested riding the range
below the breaks, thinking that the likeliest place for
an attack.

Lobo let his sons feed and then he let them play.
They had acted well considering that they were young.
Rising, now, he snarled a warning. He must start them
back to the cover of the high country. They must learn
that a full belly is dangerous and that the price of life
is vigilance in the wilderness.

Leaping off toward the barren hills, he sounded his
call. Reluctantly the pups followed. Not one of them
relished a long, hard run on a full stomach. Lobo
dropped back and lunged at one who was trailing. The
veal gorged pup tumbled over, yelping in pain as
Lobo's teeth cut into his tender shoulder. After that
there was no lagging and the pack ran heavily for
several hours.

Lobo did not let them stop just inside the breaks,
but drove them on into the depths of the broken country, where thick forest and deep canyons offered a safe
lolling place. The hide-out would last for several days
and the king wolf wanted to take no chances.

When Lobo halted it was in a deep forest of spruce.
The place angered him because it was an ideal spot for

He hurled himself at his mate

raising a pack of pups and it reminded him of the trim she-wolf Bart had lured from him.

Morning found the pack sleeping off the effects of their orgy near a clear stream which afforded water. The king wolf would not have slept had he known that two grey shadows had paused in the late moonlight and watched the pack for a long time. One of the forms, a slender, graceful shadow, had led the bigger one away after considerable coaxing. And through her persuasiveness Bart missed a chance to end the depredations of the pack for he could easily have destroyed them all in their meat-glutted condition.

But Bart was in the flush of first love, and duty was forgotten. He had followed the she-wolf on into the shadows of the timber where they had hunted rabbits.

That morning Parsons and Tex Lee went out with Charlie to ride.

"We better take a circle up along the breaks," Tex suggested.

Charlie shook his head. "The lower country is best," he said shortly.

And there was nothing to do about it but to go to the lower pastures if the two cattle men wanted to ride with their hunter. Charlie rode along in silence, his eyes on the ground and his feet hanging out of his stirrups.

A mile above a little meadow where a tiny lake

glistened in the morning sun and the tall grass nodded under a load of dew, Charlie halted and got down from his horse. He examined the ground carefully for some minutes, then without a word, got back on his horse and headed down country.

Parsons and Tex followed impatiently. They were sure nothing would be found so far from the breaks, but they knew from experience that their hunter was not one to waste time on wild chases that were certain to prove fruitless.

Charlie jogged ahead, his legs bumping up and down against the stirrups. He was all eagerness inside and all stolid calm outwardly. He knew they were coming to a kill; the heavy tracks he had just examined indicated that a pack had been returning that way from a feed.

Riding out into the little meadow where Lobo and his sons had held their orgy of killing he halted. Silently he sat like a bronze statue looking over the trampled grass. Five carcasses lay in the sun—five torn and partly devoured calves.

Parsons and Tex spurred forward and leaped from their horses. Slowly Charlie got down. He was as eager as they, but his iron will kept him back. One at a time he silently inspected the carcasses.

"This has to be stopped. It will not happen again!" Parsons straightened and faced Tex.

"It's costly business," Tex admitted looking toward Charlie.

"Did you hear, Charlie—this is to be stopped, now!" Parsons was beside himself with anger.

"Jerry fought Lobo for a whole season and never got him," the Indian said smoothly.

Parsons walked to another carcass and bent over it. Straightening he shouted. "Come here!"

Tex and Charlie advanced and stood over the mangled calf. Parsons pointed to the fang rips on the calf's flanks, then looked the hunter squarely in the eye. Charlie seemed hardly to look but his black eyes darkened.

"You never killed that dog," Parsons said evenly his first anger having cooled. "Charlie, you have made a big mistake and a costly one for me."

Charlie nodded. He was angry with himself and more than angry with the brute he had trusted. "I get him," he said shortly his face a mask.

"You better do it before he makes another kill like this one." Parsons turned to his horse and mounted.

During the next four weeks Charlie worked day and night. He brought up an old horse and killed it. He smoked a dozen traps and spread them on all the cross trails, using smoked gloves to make the sets. The horse was killed and quartered and cut into squares of a size that would make one tasty mouthful for a wolf.

These squares were scattered in the meadows near the breaks. They were just horse meat, no poison; dainty morsels to tempt hungry appetites.

For several days the horse meat was scattered. Then came a halt and in a few days more the same thing was tried again. Tex Lee grunted with disapproval as he cut up the meat for Charlie to scatter.

"What's the use of putting out baits that have no poison in them?" he demanded of one of the men.

"No use, except to keep us chopping up this old horse," the man growled. "Looks to me like that buck Indian has gone off his nut."

"Parsons still thinks he's all right," Tex said slitting another piece of meat. "And each piece has to have a strip of fat."

Charlie was standing at the corner of his cabin and heard this conversation, but he said nothing. He was looking away toward Chimney Rock wondering what the great breed dog he had lost was doing. The pack had not ravished the Circle Bar range for two weeks, but word had come up from the other side of the mountain that a kill had been made over there.

Parsons appeared from down at the corrals. He had just come in from the lower country.

"Any news?" Tex asked.

"Yes, the Flying K lost four calves Monday night. I rode over and talked to their foreman. We went out

and examined the kills." Parsons eyes rose and met the
black ones of the hunter. "One of the calves was hamstrung by a wolf with one broken fang."

Charlie returned his boss' gaze with a blank stare,
but he shifted his weight from against the cabin and
walked toward the corrals.

"That dog is sure raising ned," Tex said when
Charlie was out of hearing.

"There has to be action around here pretty soon or
we get another hunter," Parsons stated flatly.

"Now you're talking sense," Tex said dropping his
knife.

"No; we're not lying down on him till I say the
word." The boss turned and walked to his own cabin.

Charlie stopped at the horse corral and looked at
his saddle for a long time. He could not do much of
anything, but he wanted to get away from camp. He
had ridden hard and had lain on ridges for hours, but
he had never sighted Bart; neither, for that matter,
had he sighted Lobo.

Dragging the saddle from its peg he started toward
his pony. He would ride up into the breaks and stay
over night there. The kill on the other side of the
mountain meant nothing. Charlie was sure the pack
would be back within a week because the rough country
was on the Stuben Canyon side and the pack would
choose a hide-out there.

Without much enthusiasm he headed his pony up the slope and jogged along. Mid-summer had brought some changes to the range. Several frosts had ripened the tall grass and already the slopes were beginning to darken with purple and gold blossoms, sign that the brief burst of summer was passing.

Charlie could not keep up the hatred with which he had started this hunt to end the life of the dog that had been his constant comrade for two seasons. He realized that this, more than anything else, was the reason he had not done more to clear the range of the killer.

It was true that in the past weeks the Circle Bar had escaped the raiders, but other ranges had suffered. Two had been heard from and likely more would send in their word of killings.

Charlie slapped a big horse-fly that had settled upon the neck of his cayuse. He would ride the breaks country clear back to the heavy timber and trust to luck. If he sighted Bart he promised himself grimly that he would shoot to kill. An end to soft feeling. Bart had earned his fate.

CHAPTER VI

Beyond the Breaks

B ART and his slender mate had run far beyond the horizon of the world they had both known. At first the big dog let his mate lead. Soon he swung ahead and they raced on. He was striking out into new worlds, always heading north and a little west, following the hog backs and ridges of the Colorado Rockies, keeping high along the blue-green timber line.

Lobo was forgotten. Charlie's strong friendship no longer pulled as it had the first week away from his cabin. True it was that the grey one had trouble every time they sighted the lights of some lone rancher in one of the little valleys that cut back toward the high country. Bart would remember his training, his responsibilities, that old comradeship, and try to strike off toward the habitation below. Always the slender she-wolf would stand in the way. Always she won, and they would race on with Bart lagging a little.

Sioux Charlie's training had been weak in one respect. He had sought to develop in Bart that streak of savage nature he had inherited from his father. Bart was an apt pupil—he cared for no man except Charlie, he was a savage killer, but one step from the wild thing he was fast becoming. Charlie's work had been too thorough.

Soon the shifty ways of the she-wolf began to fix themselves upon Bart. Instead of running in the open, he now skirted cover and slid from one timber patch to another, avoiding the open in the daytime and sliding across it swiftly at night.

But through it all Bart held to part of his training. He never pulled down cattle or colts; his food consisted of rabbits and squirrels. The she-wolf grew dismayed at this and sulked when Bart refused to kill. The big dog ignored her sulking, for here, too, he had been trained well in a habit not to be broken in a few weeks.

The run to the north ended on a ridge high up in the Teton Mountains. Bart sat on a ledge overlooking a desolation he had never known before. Far below them a light twinkled and winked, marking the cabin of a rancher. A great longing swept over the big dog.

Three weeks had passed since they had left the head
of Stuben Canyon and again he was remembering.

The she-wolf sat at his side uneasily licking a paw
which she had bruised on a rock. She seemed to sense
the feeling of her mate.

Bart stood erect and faced southward. She rose, too,
and stood beside him shouldering close. Something was
wrong. The natural urge to hunt a home spot for her
puppies had not come; she was barren and she knew
it. And now her mate was facing into the country that
she feared. Bart moved off down the slope without
looking back. The slim, grey one hesitated a minute,
then followed.

Once headed back Bart struck out eagerly. He was
going home and he did not want to halt. Running
silently with powerful strides he forced his mate to
her best pace.

Daybreak found them well to the south and still
running. The grey one thrust her foam-flecked muzzle
up alongside of Bart's massive jaws and whined through
her teeth. Bart slowed to a trot and stopped. The slender
wolf at his side was tiring. Swinging into a dense growth
of balsam he halted and looked at her. She stretched out
on the ground and closed her eyes. Bart lay down, too.
He would rest that day but he knew that night would
find him again swinging southward.

With the coming of night they were off again, swerving from their course only long enough to run down a big snow-shoe rabbit that leaped from a thicket. Bart cut in from one side of the thicket and the she-wolf from the other. The rabbit raced like mad but before he had reached a second clump of bushes the two had overtaken him and had divided his carcass between them at one slashing thrust.

The taste of blood made the she-wolf long for the hunt. She kept a sharp watch for game and when a doe leaped from the cover of an aspen grove she swerved and charged after the fleeing animal. Down the slope they raced wildly. Bart halted and watched, his fangs bared and his teeth shining in the starlight. The doe fled with long, leaping bounds straight toward the protection of a big buck who was feeding below.

The buck heard her coming and snorted. Planting himself in the tall grass he swung his eight point antlers till they swept the ground. The she-wolf saw him and swung in a wide circle yelping for Bart. Her hunting blood was hot and she wanted to fight. Bart came leaping down the slope, but he did not attack the buck. Instead he hurled himself at his mate and sent her rolling on the ground.

The she-wolf got up panting and whimpering. She was surprised but not angry. Bart was her master and he was beginning to make it known. It was plain that he did not want her to chase deer. With a submissive look she dropped in at his side and they raced on toward the south.

Seven days of running and resting brought them back to the breaks above Stuben Canyon and Bart eagerly headed across the canyon toward the home ranch. This time he led the way down into the canyon and out again. The she-wolf grew truly troubled. She feared the results of this night's run and would have turned back had she dared, but Bart was savagely dominant now and she was afraid of him. By nine o'clock they broke over the rim above the Circle Bar summer camp. Bart halted and sat down to gaze through the starlight upon his old home. Caution had come into his ways now, and held him back.

The she-wolf whimpered and coaxed but Bart sat and looked. A light appeared in Sioux Charlie's cabin and Bart stirred restlessly. Charlie would be cooking a late supper. Bart longed to run down, to leap against the door, to rush in and spring up against his old master, but another and stronger pull held him back.

The door of the hunter's cabin opened and a band of light flooded the yard. The she-wolf leaped up and sprang back. Bart growled reassuringly and she lay down. The door closed and Bart got to his feet.

Down at the corrals a man was unsaddling his horse. He dragged the saddle over to the corral and hung it up. Bart sniffed the wind that blew up from the corral.

The man was Tex Lee. With a guttural whine Bart started down the hill. He did not look back at the she-wolf and she did not rise. She would wait for him.

Bart trotted down to the edge of the clearing which contained the buildings. He was crossing the yard as Tex Lee came from the corrals. Tex did not see the dog until he was within a few yards of him. When he did he halted and his right hand shot to his side. It came away glinting dully. The dim light was pierced by a stabbing flash. Twice Tex's gun flamed. Its roar woke echoes in the silent rims above.

With the first flash of fire Bart felt a searing pain across his shoulder and at the second he was away, up the hill.

Tex Lee stood motionless, his smoking gun in his hand. "Missed him at twenty feet," he grunted.

Sioux Charlie appeared at his door. He had been expecting this to happen and he grimly waited for Tex to come up.

"It was that dog of yours and I missed," he called to the hunter.

"You shoot poor," Charlie said stepping out into the starlight. "I will do better."

Bart ran wildly for a half mile, his shoulder burning cruelly. The she-wolf had fled ahead of him but she circled and overtook him. Bart paid no attention to her.

He was experiencing a new sensation—the fear of man. Now he knew how it felt to have the hand of civilization against him. A savage rage boiled in his breast.

Heading straight toward the meadows at the foot of Chimney Rock he ran without purpose. Reaching the last pasture below the breaks he halted and lay down. The she-wolf crawled up close and Bart let her lick the ragged wound on his shoulder.

For several hours they rested while the slim grey one tended the wound as best she could; at last Bart rose and they were off again. The she-wolf would soon learn that Bart's welcome would make him hers indeed. No longer would he be drawn to lighted cabins.

Suddenly Bart leaped aside and shoved the wolf out of the trail. He had recognized a trap set where two paths crossed. Carefully he approached the set, lying flat on his belly and pawing himself ahead. Reaching out with one big forepaw he swept the ground with a sidewise motion. His paw struck steel and he moved it more slowly. Suddenly there was a snap and the air was filled with dry leaves and twigs. Bart was making use of an old trick, one Charlie had trained him to work successfully in the days back at the cabin.

The she-wolf leaped in terror as the jaws of the trap rose into sight. Bart got up and stood smelling the closed and harmless steel jaws. He coaxed the she-wolf but she would not come near the trap. After five minutes of fooling with the trap and kicking sticks and stones over it to show his disdain Bart trotted away.

A quarter of a mile farther on the wolf swung from her mate's side and snapped up a square of meat that lay beside the trail. Instantly Bart was upon her snarling and snapping at the morsel. The she-wolf thought he was trying to snatch it from her for himself and gulped it down at a swallow. Bart attacked her savagely; he knew what that sweet morsel of horse meat was and he wanted to impress on her the danger of eating it.

The she-wolf leaped aside and ran a few steps. At her feet lay another choice bit of horse meat with a strip of fat on one side. Greedily she snatched at it but Bart was too quick for her. He tore it from her lips and tossed it aside, then hurled himself against her. She went down yelping and kicking.

Bart stood over her and watched. A great fear was clutching at his heart. He had worked with Charlie in setting hundreds of baits and he knew what to expect from one of them. He himself had gulped down a tempting square of horse meat Charlie had prepared and had been deathly sick. The square had been doped to cure him and it had done its work.

Then he remembered coming upon a wolf who had eaten a bait; he had watched the brute writhe on the ground until its legs stiffened and it could only roll its eyes and froth at the mouth. Now he watched the she-wolf closely. She was not sick, but she was angry and sullen. Bart tried to soothe her and when he failed to soften her mood, he raised his hunting cry and struck off in search of rabbits.

His mate followed sulkily for a time, but when a big jack-rabbit broke cover, she joined her mate in tearing the jack to shreds. The struggle over the bait she soon forgot in the fun of running down jacks—she forgot, but Bart did not. With a purpose he shifted the hunt toward the breaks away from the meadows below.

He had met another threat against their life, their liberty, and was pushed one step farther from the bonds of domestication.

Down at the Circle Bar Ranch Sioux Charlie had not gone into his cabin. Lighting his pipe he sat with his back against the logs of the outer wall and thought deeply. Tomorrow he would throw out poison bait. The pack had fed on choice cuts for long enough, cuts that contained no government poison.

One of the Circle Bar meadows had been visited for another kill, and Charlie had been expecting Bart's visit. This latest kill had brought down three calves, close to the ranch buildings, so close that it looked like an attempt to taunt the owner of the Circle Bar. Parsons was desperate and had hinted that he was sending out for another hunter.

Charlie's pipe went out. He had been working for the Circle Bar and Parsons for many years and he had always been looked upon as the best hunter in the state. Now that Bart had gone bad, had turned traitor, Charlie was out of favor; more than likely Parsons would fire him when the new man arrived.

The Indian sat erect. A long-drawn howl came hurtling down the wind, a threat and a challenge. Charlie could not mistake that deep-chested cry. It was Bart. He rose and entered the cabin. He took his rifle from its peg over the door.

That call might mean a kill, and Charlie determined to prevent it. Hurrying down to the corrals he caught his pony and saddled her. He had only starlight to shoot by, but he might, by riding, prevent slaughter.

The call had come from up near the breaks and Charlie headed that way.

Lobo's scruff rose and he snapped savagely

CHAPTER VII

The Return of the Killer

BART and the she-wolf ranged along the breaks that night, running rabbits and playing tag in and out of the dense black shadows of the spruce and the lighter patches of meadow.

They had been chasing a big jack and had just divided his carcass between them. Bart was not hungry and had satisfied himself by shaking the hind quarters of the rabbit and tossing it into the air. He was about to pounce upon the gory toy when he heard a familiar sound. Tensing his muscles he listened and sniffed.

The scent was a familiar one; it was Charlie and his cayuse. Bart leaped back into the dark shade beneath a balsam and waited. The she-wolf had picked up the scent, too, and was shrinking into the black cover.

Charlie and his horse rode into view through the star-light. The Indian was riding listlessly, his shoulders hunched forward as though doing something he knew was useless, but doing it because he could not help himself.

Bart checked a sudden desire to rush out and bark. His experience at the cabin had made him wary even of his old master. The ache at his shoulder kept warning him to go slow in showing himself.

With a hesitant and shifty movement he edged out of the blackness. At that moment luck, in the form of a dog coyote, trotted into the open from the windward. The coyote had smelled Bart's torn rabbit and he was hungry. He halted in the open, a dim patch against the spruce and balsams.

Charlie saw the coyote instantly. He was not sure it was a coyote because the light was bad but he knew it was either that or a wolf. Like a flash he whipped his rifle from the saddle horn and took a snap shot. The fire from his gun and the crashing report sent Bart leaping back into the cover. As he fled he looked back and saw a struggling form in the tall grass. Charlie's aim was still deadly even in less than half light. Bart crowded the willing grey one in a race for the breaks.

He could not have known why he ran, unless it was the ache in his shoulder and the experience at the camp.

One thing only was certain; Bart was gun-shy now, and gun-wise.

Charlie dismounted and turned the coyote over with his foot. He grunted in disgust. Here was only a petty thief, and he had thought for a moment that he was bringing down the true culprit. Swinging the coyote up behind his saddle, he tied it on and continued his circle, doggedly determined to ride out the night.

Daylight was painting the east a burnished silver as he rode into camp. He threw the carcass of the coyote over the corral poles, loosed his horse, and walked slowly to his cabin.

Breakfast was merely a recall of habit with him that morning. He fried bacon and made flapjacks without thinking once of what he was doing. He had just washed the last dish when his boss' voice greeted him.

"Morning, Charlie," Parsons said.

Charlie grunted and stacked the dry tin plate he had been wiping in its place.

Parsons entered the cabin and sat down. He cleared his throat as though reluctant to start.

Charlie washed his hands and dumped the contents of the wash pan out through the door; then he too sat down.

"The boys are riding me pretty hard. They think you aren't trying, or else that you've lost your wolf sense," Parsons began.

Charlie grunted again, his face a mask.

"After seeing that dog of yours again right after this last kill they are doing a lot of talking."

"I let them talk," Charlie spoke softly but his voice held a touch of bitterness.

"They want a new hunter," Parsons stated simply.

Charlie got up and walked to the window.

"I have made this proposition to them. We will give you a chance to finish with your bait sets."

"Then I go—if no wolf takes them or if Bart is too wise?" Charlie asked the question as though making a statement.

"That's about the size of it." Parsons rose. "I hope you get the whole pack, Charlie."

"And them in the Cattle Association?" Charlie wanted to know the worst.

"They insist upon black-listing you if you fall down. The story of your dog has leaked out." Parsons had not intended to tell this.

Charlie turned from the window. "I sleep," was all he said, and crossed the room to his bunk.

Parsons left and walked down to the corrals. He saw the coyote and noticed that Charlie's horse had been out late. A look of sympathy came into his grim eyes. The hunter was doing his best.

Charlie did not sleep. He lay looking up at the smoke-grimed logs, the ceiling of his cabin. The logs were split and matched after a fashion. Where they were not fitted closely the dirt from the roof showed through, and water-stains darkened the wood.

If he failed to get the killers this time he would be through as a hunter. The Cattle Association, linked as it was with all the associations in the west, would see to it that he did not get another job.

Had Charlie been all Indian he might have rolled over and gone to sleep with a shrug of his heavy shoulders, but his father had been the best hunter in the Rockies, and had been proud of it. Charlie had always been the envy of lesser wolf-men, and now he was about to be branded a failure.

His thoughts allowed him but little sleep that day, and in the evening dusk he rose and went outside. There would be no supper for him. Food could wait. He took his rifle with him and walked down to another cabin in which, because it was cool, his baits were lying spread out on the floor.

Charlie sat down, drew a slender knife from one pocket and a can from the other. Pulling on a pair of smoked gloves, he picked up one of the squares of horse meat and slit it carefully. A measure of poison from the can he placed in the slit, and pressed the flesh tight over it.

For half an hour he worked silently in the moon-light. The can of poison was empty. He gathered up the baits and put them in a smoked wrapper. In the corral, a step or two away, he caught his cayuse and saddled him.

Charlie rode to the meadows below the breaks where he had scattered the first chunks of horse meat. Carefully he tossed out his baits as he rode along. He knew that many a coyote would gulp down those deadly morsels, but what he hoped was that some of Bart's pack, if Bart's it was, would be caught in a hungry and careless mood.

After the baits were tossed he went the rounds of his trap sets. When he came to the one his dog had sprung he got down and examined the ground. Rising he smiled grimly. The joke was on him. He had trained Bart to avoid traps, and he had broken him of eating baits; now the dog was against him and had the advantage. In the grey dawn he mounted his horse and rode out.

He passed several riders from the Circle Bar and they scarcely waved at him. They were beginning to treat him coldly because he had failed to run down the pack.

On the way back to camp he rode through a patch of late berries, and a cinnamon bear rose to look him over. Charlie sat on his startled cayuse and watched the bear. He had no intention of shooting the animal; it was only a cub. The cinnamon bear grinned in a friendly way and scooped in a handful of berries. He crammed the ripe fruit into his mouth and ate it noisily.

Charlie had always felt a friendliness toward cinnamon bears. They are harmless and seldom turned out to be killers of stock, and they are the most humane of all wild animals. This youngster seemed to know that the Indian was his friend. He went on smearing his face with berries and grunting.

Charlie touched his cayuse with his heel and whistled shrilly. The bear dropped from sight in the bushes and ambled away up the hill.

Riding on down to the cabin the hunter turned his pony loose and walked to his cabin. All he could do now was to wait for his sets to work. Today he would sleep, but along toward sundown he would go out and pick a look-out from which he might get a rifle shot that would count.

Sundown found him on a ridge overlooking one of the lower meadows. Six white-faced cows were feeding on the ripe grass, and six sturdy calves played or fed beside them. The calves were huskies with almost a summer's growth on them. Every one was a high grade animal and valuable. Charlie began reckoning up the cost of the summer's killings. It ran into big money—more than he had saved in his whole life as a hunter.

Charlie set down the figures he summed up in his mind. With a stump of a pencil and a dirty bit of paper he painstakingly wrote out the amount; he shoved the penciled scrap into his pocket. He would pay what he could of the damage. Then quit—unless the baits worked.

Charlie sat up straight and gripped his rifle. A she-wolf had burst from the timber running madly, leaping over fallen logs and bunches of tall grass. At her heels raced a great dog, his dog, Bart!

Charlie's gun flashed up and he pulled a bead, not on the wolf, but on the dog. His aim did not steady as it usually did. He must follow the rushing form below. The she-wolf darted straight for the nearest calf. As she did so the dog at her heels caught up with her and headed her roughly back across the clearing. Charlie held his fire. The wolf was between him and the dog. Seeing that he was about to miss his chance he squeezed the trigger.

The she-wolf leaped into the air and staggered around in a half-circle. Her mate crowded her close and shoved her into the cover of a clump of willows.

Charlie raced across the meadow. At the clump of willows he halted. The dog and his mate had escaped. Blood clots on the grass and weeds pointed up the slope, and showed which way they had fled.

"That was almost good, feller," Charlie muttered.

The white-faced cows and their calves stood watching him suspiciously from the edge of the timber where they had fled when the she-wolf charged upon them.

"Like his father, Old Bart; he mates with a wolf," Charlie said aloud.

A magpie sailed down into the meadow with a hopeful glassy eye cocked for food. Finding nothing he rose and flew with a dipping swing toward the upper meadows. He had seen a staggering grey wolf head that way; he would watch the course of the stricken animal. His meals depended upon such watchfulness.

Charlie knew he could accomplish nothing by staying on the ridge so he caught his cayuse and rode toward camp.

One thing kept rising in his thoughts and that was the way Bart had headed the she-wolf away from the calf. He shrugged his shoulders and put it out of his mind. Later that night Bart would gather his pack and descend upon this same herd, perhaps, perhaps some other, and lead the kill.

Charlie said nothing to any of the men at the corrals when he got in. That he had missed a wolf at a hundred yards would only make the boys more certain he had lost his cunning as a hunter.

He prepared his supper and ate moodily. After the dishes were washed he went outside and smoked his pipe. From up on a distant ridge he heard a mournful cry and wondered grimly if Bart were grieving for a lost mate. His pipe began to draw water and taste bitter, so he knocked it out with an impatient thump of the bowl on his heel. Rising he went inside and lay upon his bunk. Presently Parsons came in.

"One of the boys sighted Lobo and his pack today. They were heading down through the breaks. It was Kelley and he is a rotten shot with a rifle. He missed at less than a hundred yards." Parsons spoke abruptly, but there was a note of kindness in his voice.

Charlie raised himself on one elbow. This was good news. The pack would pass through his bait sets and he might have some luck. Parsons seemed to sense his thoughts.

"It's about time you had a break, Charlie; I hope you get it tonight." The boss rose and turned toward the door.

"I want to make you an offer," Charlie spoke from the bunk.

Parsons turned and stood in the center of the room.

Charlie reached behind his bunk and fumbled with a loose board. In a few minutes he produced a tobacco can and a sack. Opening the can he shook out a roll of bills, while from the sack he emptied a pile of silver coins.

"Bart has caused a lot of killing and beef is like money. You take what I have saved and give some to the other outfits. I would be square." Charlie's words came slowly and evenly.

Parsons looked at the money a long time; then he looked his hunter in the eye. "That's white, Charlie, but I would not take that money under any circumstances. You just forget about past kills." Without another word he left the cabin.

Charlie put the money back and lay down again. He had not given up his plan to square himself.

Outside Parsons whistled under his breath absentmindedly as he made his way to his own cabin. The boys might kick and the Association black-list Charlie, but the Indian was square—all through.

CHAPTER VIII

Lobo Trains His Pack

LOBO was fast making a finished pack of his four sons. They killed now without playing, and many times they killed for pure love of slaughter. Lobo had seen many years in the cow country and had learned much. Year after year he had found the hunt more difficult. The higher ranges bordering on inaccessible reaches of timber and canyon were the only safe places left. The lower country with its ranches and irrigated pastures was now closed to him and his pack.

Time was when he had ravaged the valleys and plains, but the coming of the farmer and the dairy man and the sheep man had ended that. There were mesh fences cutting across the runways, and Lobo knew that those high wire barriers formed death traps. Summer was easy for him, but winter always brought famine and hunger.

The tang of fall in the air made him moody and savage. His jowls were beginning to fringe with grey and he did not look forward to hardships with the carelessness of winters past. In the lower country summer still smiled and harvest was just beginning, but in the high country the brief summer was at an end, and the briefer fall had come.

Soon the cattle would be started downward to make sure no early blizzard caught them. The herds would be guarded by armed riders by day and by night to keep them from straying back to the range. Then the hunting would be hard and the killings would be few. Deer would be left for a while, though the does, too, had started down. Lobo knew that he and his pack would have to fight for their venison when nothing was left to them but the bucks.

The closing in of that circle of safe wilderness had taught the king wolf many things. He was trap-wise and bait-wise and he meant that his sons should be as wary as he was. Once Lobo had been caught in a coyote trap and had broken a fang tearing himself loose from the steel jaws. The trap had been too light to hold him but it had taught him to avoid sets. Back in his dim past he had gulped down a lump of fat and had suffered agonies till he vomited the burning ball of grease. There, too, he had been lucky. An amateur had made the bait and had figured that the more strychnine he used the better, so Lobo had been made sick enough to throw up the poison.

Now the great wolf stood looking down over the slopes at the foot of Chimney Mountain. Behind him were the towering ridges above timberline, mantled in new snow even to the first stunted and wind warped cedars. He was restless and eager to descend with his pack to the pastures below but the hour was too early.

One of his sons trotted up to him and smelled at his gaunt side. Lobo's coarse scruff rose and he snapped savagely at the dog wolf. The youngster leaped back, grinning wickedly as he did so. He was the venturesome pup who had tried to steal the she-wolf from his father earlier in the summer. Lobo glared at him fiercely. This young killer was marked for leader when Lobo could no longer handle the pack. Nature had taken care of that.

The youngster was powerful of chest and long of leg. He had the neck and head of a killer and he had courage. Lobo had already felt his will on several occasions, and more than once he had been forced to hurl him to the ground and stand over him.

If Lobo knew that this dog wolf was to take his place he did not let it interfere with his son's training. That was but the law of the wilderness, and Lobo was only a part of its great scheme of life and death. He could not do otherwise.

As dusk began to settle, the leader of the pack trotted down the slope. His sons ran and snapped at his side. When they reached the meadows below the breaks the king wolf lengthened his stride. A savage hatred was swelling within him, a lust to kill, not because he was hungry, but because fall was in the air and winter was coming and above all a touch of stiffness was beginning to creep into his bones.

Lobo was not failing in health; the husky dog wolf running ahead of the other three knew that. He was still a match for any brute on the range; but there was no play left in him, only savage lust and grim wariness.

Down the slope they ran, swerving within striking distance of cover, always watching to the side and ahead. The timber wolf is not built to look back and to the side as is the rabbit who is hunted. The wolf is a hunter and his eyes are set well front. But the tightening grip of man on the wild country has forced the hunter to take on the role of hunted, and to look back and to the side.

Not that Lobo allowed men to run him out of his native country. He feared them and avoided them, but he dared them, too. This night was to see a piece of his daring. He was swinging downward toward the cabins of the Circle Bar. He would make his kill among the summer calves kept close to the corrals.

Racing on, the pack swung into the larger meadows. They passed several herds of cows and calves without looking at them. They knew that at the end of the run there would be blood and slaughter. At the end of all Lobo's runs was red slaughter. Silently they ran, their red tongues lolling out across their slender fangs, and their ribs rising and falling evenly.

One of the dog wolves yelped and slid to a halt. Lobo broke his stride and turned with a snarl. The youngster had discovered a square of meat, fresh and tempting. Several days before he had snatched up a like morsel and gulped it down. That time Lobo had been running a ridge above and had not seen him. The youngster knew that more squares were lying about; there had been that other time.

Crushing down on the square he looked around for another. Like a screaming projectile Lobo was upon him, snatching at the meat. The pup gulped and swallowed the sweet chunk, leaping clear of his leader's fangs as he did so. Frantically Lobo whirled from one to the other of the pack slashing them cruelly in an attempt to drive them from the little meadow. They went with wonder in their hard eyes.

The youngster who had gulped the tasty square of horse meat ran with his eyes on the grass, eager to snatch up another bite. He found no more, nor did the others. Slowly the strip of fat melted in the wolf's

Bart snarled and snatched the fish

stomach and the juices began to run out of the lean part. The dog wolf missed a stride, then caught himself. He missed another and a whine rose in his throat. Something was gripping at his vitals, searing him the length of his sinewy frame.

Lobo whirled and came back. He reached the stricken pup as the big fellow went down, his lips flecked with foam and his eyes glaring. Struggling to his feet the youngster tried to run but collapsed again. Lobo nosed him rumbling deep in his throat, all his roughness vanished and he licked the prostrate pup eagerly, trying to get him up.

He could not help the stricken wolf. Sioux Charlie had used government poison, deadly and sure. Unlike strychnine it did not drive its victim in search of water, though there was a crying need and a burning thirst. It killed quickly, as humanely as a killing can be accomplished.

Lobo stood over his son until the dog wolf ceased quivering; then he sat down, his great head hanging low. The other three stood watching uneasily, unable to understand this strange happening. Vaguely they knew that something had stretched their brother out and that he had not moved since falling.

The old wolf got to his feet. He had seen this happen before and knew that the youngster would never follow again; that his pack was reduced to three huskies.

Without a glance backward he trotted away. In a few minutes the pack was running again, swiftly and silently, toward the Circle Bar pasture.

Lobo did not swerve from his purpose. He would kill within the shadow of the ranch buildings that night. He would show the men he hated that he could not be stopped.

The calf pasture was protected by a pole fence but this did not stop the pack. When they came to it they leaped over the top rail and burst into the cry of the kill. Racing and slashing they descended upon the summer calves, a motherless herd Parsons had brought in when larkspur and bloat-weed had killed the cows.

The calves scattered, bellowing in terror, while the wolves hurled themselves upon them. Lobo cut down his calf close to the fence, his savage charge bowling the terrified veal over on its side. The calves were big but the pack did not mind that. They were killing for the pure lust of blood.

At the cabins Parsons and Charlie heard the commotion and ran out into the night with their rifles. Tex Lee and two of the cowboys joined them. At the calf pasture they sighted the grey forms and opened fire, but into the air because of the calves. The grey shadows vanished, and could be heard yelping as they raced through the timber.

Parsons let himself over the fence and almost landed on the carcass of a calf. The animal was still alive and struggling. Charlie had leaped over the fence at his boss' heels and stood by while Parsons dispatched the calf with his revolver.

Up the mountain side a cry rang out. It was scornful and cruel, a challenge and a threat. Lobo was hurling defiance down the wind.

Parsons wiped his forehead and produced a flashlight. He played the beam from the light over the kill. Both he and Charlie bent forward. On the ham of the calf were slashes where the killer's fangs had ripped seeking a tendon. Parsons straightened.

"That broken fang again, Charlie," he said in disgust.

Charlie grunted and straightened. He was angry through and through, but he had nothing to say.

Tex Lee came over and Parsons flashed the light on the carcass. Tex looked and said nothing, but it was plain that he wanted to say a lot.

The men went back to their cabins in silence. Charlie knew, however, that plenty would be said when the men got out of his hearing. Bart would be bitterly berated and every man would blame the hunter for having kept a dog that was part wolf.

Charlie went to his own cabin and sat a long time with the light burning. He was expecting a visit from Parsons. The boss did not come for the better part of an hour, but he did come. He had been in the bunk house with his men talking over the situation.

When he came in he closed the door and sat down grimly.

"Bad business, Charlie," he said at last.

"Yes, and with Bart trained to know traps and baits," Charlie spoke straightforwardly.

"Yes," Parsons nodded.

"You should take the money," Charlie spoke slowly.

"No," Parsons shook his head. "It isn't the money now; it's a matter of making the range safe and of getting that bloody brute out of the way." Parsons got to his feet and pounded the table with his fist. "He is making sport of us, coming down into our yard and making his kills."

"When are you moving the cows down?" Charlie spoke without enthusiasm.

"Pretty soon. If this keeps up we will be forced out in a week."

"I do not look for much from the baits," Charlie said.

"Well, something has to be done. Think hard to-night, Charlie." Parsons stood up and left the cabin.

Charlie knew Parsons had not said what he came to say. The boss was too fine a man to let himself be forced into firing any of his help until they had had every chance.

The men would have made demands for a new hunter. Charlie knew that. And he knew as well how forceful the demands must have been that night.

Lying down on his bunk he tried to think of a way out. The only solution was to leave all the money he had and go. They would get a new wolf-man and if he went they would have to take the money. He could locate far up in the breaks at the foot of Chimney Rock and continue to hunt for the killer.

Charlie knew where there was a cabin and he had provisions enough to last him several months. He hated to think of leaving the home he had lived in for so many years, but most of all he hated the disgrace. He had been beaten, and, worst of all, by his own dog and a pack of whelp wolves.

Wearily he closed his eyes and dozed off to sleep to dream of meeting Bart in hand to hand conflict and killing him. He woke with a start and lay thinking of that dream. In it he had seen himself bending over the dead Bart trying to wake him up. The dream was so real he did not sleep again for hours.

CHAPTER IX

At the Foot of the Engelmann Spruce

BART coaxed and bullied his grey mate across the meadows and through the timber toward the breaks. She was staggering from a wound in her side. Loss of blood made her sick and weak but fear drove her on, fear and the big dog at her side. Sioux Charlie had pulled a little fine and his bullet had cut low across the breast of the she-wolf.

When they struck the heavy timber Bart began looking for a hide-out. While the grey one rested, panting and whining after each short run, Bart would dart away and search for a safe place for her to rest.

The spot he finally selected was a dirt cave formed by the fall of a giant Engelmann spruce. Its roots, bedded on solid rock, had been unable to withstand the onslaught of a summer windstorm. When the great tree crashed to earth, it lifted a mat of needles and dirt from that rocky bed; the trunk had lodged on a ledge above. Now the forest giant strove to live with only part of its roots clinging to a thin layer of soil.

Bart led his mate under these spreading roots. At the back of the cave he pawed aside the loose dirt, clearing a spot where she might lie down. The grey one stretched out with a whimper. Bart lay beside her, and began licking her wound, rumbling deeply to re-assure her.

Late that night he left the cave alone and ran in search of food. The night was biting cold and the stars glistened frostily overhead. Bart ran with a purpose, skirting clumps of willow and juniper. After an hour of steady going he flushed a rabbit and chased it across a meadow. At the far side of the clearing he captured his game and killed it.

Swinging the dangling rabbit clear of the tall grass he headed back to the big Engelmann spruce. Halting outside the cave he tore the skin from the rabbit and then entered. With a short bark he laid the meat before his mate.

The grey one smelled of the rabbit and turned her head aside. She was far too sick to care for food. Bart scolded her with a playful snap, then began coaxing her to eat. He tore off a bit of the tender flesh and ate it, then rubbed his head against hers. Still she refused to eat. Bart knew nothing that would help her except food or sleep. She refused to eat so he crept close and laid his head beside hers in an attempt to put her to sleep.

For two hours he lay still, his eyes on the opening beneath the spreading roots, watching and listening to the breathing of the grey one. Each time she drew a long breath she whimpered and Bart stirred.

The night passed and he rose. The grey one was asleep and he did not wake her. Walking outside he looked about. Their cave was at the edge of a tiny stream which trickled over a rocky, needle-choked bed. Bart sat down and watched the trickle of water below him.

This was the second time he had met a gun in the hands of man. This time the man had been his old master. He was vaguely disturbed, he wanted to go to Charlie, but he did not dare. Every time he had been near his old pal that gun had blazed and injury had followed swiftly. Bart trotted down to the trickle of water and lapped several mouthfuls.

Straightening he saw the grey one staggering down the bank. With a leap he was at her side and licking her face. She paid no attention to him, her eyes shone glassy and her head swayed. Reaching the trickle of water she sprawled out and gulped at it as though try-

ing to pull the stream into her mouth. Shoving her
muzzle under the cold water, she let it splash over her
face.

Bart watched her closely. When she struggled to her
feet again he was at her side eager to help. She staggered back up the bank and into the cave. Stretching
out on her bed she closed her eyes. Bart examined the
rabbit; it was untouched and it was beginning to dry.
He decided that the grey one should have fresh meat
and left the cave.

Running down the slope he began a morning hunt
for small game. A squirrel escaped him by inches and
frisked to the top of a balsam where the saucy little nut-
gatherer sat scolding and chattering. But Bart ran on
paying no attention to the squirrel once the sleek morsel
of food was out of his reach. He would have liked to
carry the squirrel back to the grey one; she did not
seem to care for rabbit.

A mountain jay, crested and trim, with a bright blue
coat, shrieked at him as he raced through the timber.
The jay was making his fall pilgrimage to the high
country, dropping in before the heavy snows came to
pay a visit. He was a foolish fellow and if the urge
struck him he would stay until the mountains and
valleys were locked with snow; he might even have
to stay on waiting for spring to come.

A rock-chuck was the next morning forager Bart

saw. The chuck whistled shrilly and leaped toward the safety of a pile of slide rock. Bart swerved and charged him. The chuck frisked up on a big rock, paused a second to look scornfully down upon the big dog, then slid from sight with a last taunting whistle.

Bart paused to rest. He was not having luck in his hunting that morning. Rabbits were the best quarry and the easiest to catch, but the grey mate did not seem to want rabbit. He got up and trotted into the open.

A porcupine was feeding peacefully in the sun paying no attention to the silent world about him. He did not worry about the coming of snow. When the ground was covered and all the tender shoots buried he would climb into a spruce and feed off the thick bark of the tree. His sense of taste was dull and the strong resin flavor of the spruce bark would not worry him. It might gum his teeth but it would fill his paunch and he would live comfortably. Bart left the porcupine to feed in peace.

Across the opening he entered a grove of balsam and from there he ran on to a clump of aspens. The aspens were whispering in a musical way earning their name of "quakies." Bart did not stop long in their shade. He was worried about the grey one and eager to take her a morsel of food that would make her eat.

Coming out abruptly on a rim he looked down into

a tumbling creek. Standing in the creek was a cinnamon bear. He was scooping his paw lustily through a shallow pool and grunting loudly. Suddenly a shining and wriggling form shot out of the water and swept clear of the stream by the bear's paw. A glistening trout landed on the bank below Bart and flopped in the grass.

Bart leaped downward as the fish landed. Here was something different. Charlie was very fond of trout, and Bart had gone with him often when he caught them. Charlie had let Bart retrieve the slick trout when they came off the hook in a clump of willows or some other inaccessible place. Though Bart had never cared for the taste of fish, he wanted something different for the grey mate in the cave above.

As he pounced, the cinnamon bear floundered out of the creek and leaped toward his prize. Bart met him face to face. The bear reared up with a mighty growl. He was only half grown and not used to dogs. His black face wrinkled as he attempted to take in the situation, and he stretched a paw toward the fish. He did not want to fight, but the fish belonged to him.

Bart snarled and snatched the fish in his mouth. The bear, seeing that Bart was no friendly visitor, dropped on all fours and charged, grunting and growling. Bart leaped aside and sprang up the bank. The bear was irritated by now and gave chase, but Bart ran swiftly through the timber and disappeared into a patch of willows.

The bear sat up again, a puzzled and angry frown on his black face. He had been cheated and he had lost his breakfast. With a grunt of disgust he returned to the pool and began pawing and splashing. This time he kept an eye on the bank above but no dog appeared. When the pool was almost empty, he scooped out another fish that had been hiding under a rock at the bottom. Greedily the cub pounced on this trout and devoured it.

Bart ran straight to the hollow beneath the Engelmann spruce. Leaping inside he proudly laid the trout before the grey one. She was awake and lying where he had left her. With a weak movement of her head she shoved the trout aside; it tempted her even less than the rabbit. Bart lay down and watched her for a long time. He did not know what to do now that his last effort had failed.

That night Bart ran alone and without knowing why he was so restless. He made a wide circle and swung down toward the cabins of the Circle Bar Ranch. On a ridge above Sioux Charlie's cabin he halted and sat down, his muzzle pointed toward the stars. He was in trouble and wanted to seek aid from his old master, but he did not dare to descend to the yard where he had played in safety as a puppy.

Under the foot of the Engelmann spruce his mate was fighting against other shadows than those cast by the towering trees. She was close to the borderline between life and death. Once she tried to struggle up and get a drink but she was too weak. Sinking back she whined for Bart, but he was miles away looking down upon the starlit roof of Sioux Charlie's cabin.

At twelve o'clock a strange feeling gripped the great dog. He got up and sent his call hurtling down the wind. Not a hunting call or a challenge to battle, but a mournful, long drawn call; then he headed back to the breaks and the cave at the roots of the Engelmann spruce.

Charlie was in his cabin and heard the call. He got up from his bunk and went to the door. For a long time he stood in the dim light looking out toward the ridge above the camp. He was wondering, thinking over the happenings of the past summer, and there was a disturbing trend to his thoughts in spite of an attempt to look at the facts coldly.

He knew that Bart was up on that ridge and that he was lonesome and troubled, needing help. For a brief instant the hunter eagerly wondered if the great dog was wanting to come back and make amends.

Then Sioux Charlie remembered some other things: slaughtered calves, desertion of duty and the traitorous abuse of trust. Grimly he shut the door and crossed to his bunk. This was no time to get soft. He had, more than likely, killed Bart's mate. Now, it was up to him to kill the dog on sight.

CHAPTER X

Sioux Charlie Admits Defeat

SIOUX CHARLIE saddled his cayuse and strapped a meager pack behind the cantle. He was not going out with any enthusiasm, but rather from force of habit. He had no hope of accomplishing much with his bait sets; in fact he was thinking of something else as he jerked the cinch-strap tight and waited for the pony to let out his wind so that he could jerk again.

The hunter was pondering over a cabin high in the breaks at the foot of Chimney Rock. His wind-toughened face was drawn into serious lines of thought, and his dark eyes wandered as he looked over the Circle Bar Ranch. He would move to that cabin and wait for the coming of winter with its howling storms and its deep snows. He was eager to get away from

117

the ranch and to be alone. Sioux Charlie had given up the fight and was ready to go away and nurse his failure in the little trapper's cabin he had built years before.

With a grunt and a slap Charlie finished the saddling and walked down the wide path that led away from the corral. The pony followed him out of the yard and down the slope. Sioux Charlie headed north without a backward glance. He swung along on noiseless feet, his eyes looking far away with that steady gaze that comes to those who are always facing great horizons and wind-worn mountains.

Fall had set her stamp of gold and purple and red upon the high country. The sky seemed painted above the blue ridges of the mountains and the air held a hint of haze that was the pearl of smoke. A crispness was in the air and a tang of chill in the shadows; the sunshine was thin and not too warm. The high country was making ready for the first storm of the season. Charlie noted as he passed through a rocky dell that a few straggling cows had failed to heed the warning of the mountains and were feeding on the frost-browned grass. Charlie grunted; that was what domestication had done. The cow was too dumb to heed a clear warning; she had to be driven out by a cowboy or a lashing blizzard. Already the deer and elk had shifted ahead of the coming snows, but the range cow still clung to her sheltered nooks.

Bart watched over his dead mate

Sioux Charlie entered a meadow and plodded across its crackling grass. He was planning what he would do when he moved to his winter quarters. He had not stayed at the little cabin under the rim of Chimney Mountain for many winters and the place would need fixing. The work would have to be done before the first snow.

The hunter stopped suddenly and dropped the pony's bridle rope. He had sighted a grey form lying stretched in the grass. Leaping toward the carcass he bent eagerly forward. After a minute's scrutiny he straightened up and his eagerness vanished.

"One of the pups," he muttered. "The leader of that pack too smart."

Charlie swung the dead wolf across the saddle. He worked with a steadiness that belied his hidden feelings. When the wolf was securely trussed he headed back toward the Circle Bar. The trip back was made with his same, even, unhurried tread, but the hunter was not so calm as his pace. He had decided to give up and move to his little cabin that day.

Sioux Charlie found no one at the ranch. Grimly he skinned the wolf and stretched the hide on one of the shed walls, then returned to his own cabin and sat down to think. After a half hour of meditation he went to his bunk and began packing his slender belongings into a big roll. His bedding formed the bulk of his pack, for he had only a few personal belongings. The cooking utensils were the property of the Circle Bar Ranch, and so he left them.

From behind his bunk he took his savings. Rolling the pack outside he took the money and crossed to Parsons' cabin. He laid it beside the lamp on his boss's table, turned and stalked out. He would leave no note nor anything; he would go without apology or explanation. Parsons, he knew, would be unable to find him. After he was once settled in his trapper's cabin, Sioux Charlie would return to the ways of his boyhood—of following deadfalls and fur sets. And he would try to forget.

Leaving his pack at the door he set out toward the pasture to catch his pack animal. He would have time enough to leave the Circle Bar before Parsons or any of his crew returned. Most of the men were on the drive to the lower country and would not be riding into camp at all.

He caught the pack horse and loaded his bedding on it; then he brought up a cayuse and sacked up what supplies of bacon and canned goods he had left and tied them to his saddle. Without looking back at the little cabin he had called home for so many summers, he trailed his horses down across the slope. At the ford of Stuben Creek he turned north and headed for the rough breaks near the timber line.

Sïoux Charlie plodded upward through an afternoon that was flaming with fall colors. The brief days when the high country made its last flash of brightness before the coming of the snow held no glory for the hunter. He kept on, ignoring the scenes slowly changing as he rode upward.

By four o'clock he was on the upper edge of the Circle Bar range and well into the breaks. The country was rapidly growing rougher. Granite ridges broke through the undergrowth in bald ruggedness and the trails that crossed and recrossed toward the lower country were fainter. Here the spruces were wind-torn and bowed as though weary of fighting the storms. Sioux Charlie crossed a slide and entered a canyon. The canyon led straight toward the perpendicular walls of Chimney Rock.

Entering the canyon the man and his pack animals headed up a dry wash that showed no trail at all. The canyon was narrow, and broken rock covered its floor. The little trail wound upward for perhaps a mile then the canyon widened and a meadow appeared. At the edge of the meadow, under the sheltering boughs of three stunted spruce stood a tiny cabin. The breed led his horses to the door of the cabin and halted.

He would unpack and get his cabin in shape, then he would make a trip down the other side of the mountain for supplies enough to last him through the snow months. After that he would turn the ponies loose and let them drift down to winter range. They would be rounded up in the spring drive and he could get them then.

Sioux Charlie spent the next two days in preparing his cabin for cold weather. He chinked all the cracks and patched the old sheet iron stove with mud and chips of granite. He cleaned out the little spring at the foot of the biggest of the spruce so that his water supply would be good until the snows came.

On the second day the weather turned colder and there was a bite in the air. A wind came sweeping down from the early snows on the peaks above. It sent the dry leaves eddying around the cabin and made the ponies restless. They sensed the danger of staying longer in the high country. Charlie hauled in a supply of wood and chopped enough to last several days.

That evening found him ready for the winter. He had closed himself in from the failure he had made of his summer's hunting, and he wanted to see no human being. Except for those from whom he must buy his supplies, he would see no one until spring, and he wanted no one.

He was sitting at the door of his cabin in the dusk, his sheep-lined coat pulled tight about him, his pipe drawing damply. The sky was grey and cold with only a few of the brighter stars showing. The breed drew on his pipe and looked grimly into the night. Suddenly from a ridge above the cabin a mournful howl rose and whipped across the canyon. Sioux Charlie took his pipe from his mouth and listened, a queer tightness gripping his heart. Bart was up there on that ridge and he was not hurling defiance down the wind, he was sending a lonesome call into the night.

Bitterly Charlie knocked out his pipe. The winter would have been welcome if Bart were his comrade. He could have trapped and lived in peace with the company of his great dog. He got to his feet and shrugged his shoulders. Bart had trailed him up into the high country hoping to make up. More than likely the she-wolf had died from her wound and now the dog wanted to come home. Charlie set his mouth in a grim line and glanced to where his Winchester hung from a peg above the door. There would be no making up; he would shoot to kill on sight.

By the light of his lamp Charlie worked on one of his pack saddles. He hoped Bart would not go down; but he also hoped that he would not meet the dog. After an hour of tinkering he blew out the light and crawled into his bunk. He drifted to sleep with Bart's howl still in his ears.

The next day he set out for the nearest town across the slope. He kept away from the south side for fear of meeting Parsons or some of the Circle Bar crew.

His trip was hurried by the storm signs that were increasingly threatening. But a half day in town was all he needed, and he set out for his cabin as soon as his packs were filled.

He had bought his supplies without comment, and had answered all questions briefly. When asked where he was wintering he refused to say. The storekeeper knew hunters and did not ask many questions.

When the little train reached the base of Chimney Rock again there was a good six inches of snow on the ground. Fall had gone, the trees were bare and the underbrush rattled with a dry and frosty snap as the horses ploughed through it. Charlie stored his provisions and turned the ponies loose. They shook their shaggy sides and headed down country without delay.

Around the door of the cabin the breed found fresh dog tracks and his eyes hardened as he looked them over. Bart had paid the cabin a visit.

CHAPTER XI

The Lone Trail

FOUR times Bart returned to the cave at the foot of the fallen Engelmann spruce and each time he brought with him tempting bits of food. Once it was a chipmunk, again a cotton-tail rabbit and on the last trip a grouse that had not been swift enough to escape his savage charge.

On the fourth trip Bart laid the grouse at the slim grey one's nose. She staggered up and tore away the breast feathers and ate. Bart rumbled deep in his throat; he was strangely jubilant.

After that the slim mate recovered steadily, but slowly. The first light snow found her able to trot at Bart's side for short runs and to eat with a returning appetite.

She was gaunt and unsteady on her feet, but

she had the wiry vitality of a barren she-wolf who had failed to litter that summer. She soon took charge of Bart again and he did not visit the cabin in the little canyon at the foot of Chimney Rock after she began to run.

Hunting was fast becoming a serious problem. Bart and his grey mate foraged far along the base of the mountain. The early snows made game scarce for a week; then the little wood-folk came out again to work busily in a last brief season of harvest before the coming of that white jailer to imprison them under great drifts.

Many times they crossed the trail of Lobo and his sons, and each time Bart headed the grey one away from the wide-spread tracks. He may have had some premonition of a future meeting with Lobo, but this was not the time. He would wait until his mate was strong again.

More than once they came upon sets made by Sioux Charlie, and each time they crossed the man's trail Bart would whimper and follow the path taken by his old master. Then, indeed, would the slim she-wolf descend upon him like a grey fury to send him rushing down the slope or up the ridge away from the tracks and wherever they might lead. Bart was uneasy about the sets and he was lonesome. He feared to let Sioux Charlie see him, for he remembered what had happened the last time they met. His wolf instincts now ruled his old desire for his master.

One evening Bart and his mate were running easily down a snow slope when a big rabbit burst from the cover of a fallen log and leaped away down the hill. The grey one gave chase and Bart fell in at her side. Seeing that his mate was not yet strong enough to run down the fleet snow-shoe, Bart leaped ahead and caught the big-footed jack as he was diving into a thicket of juniper. Bart shook the limp rabbit and trotted back to where the grey one waited, panting and shaky.

They sat down and devoured the rabbit in great slashing gulps. Bart let the she-wolf have the greater part of the meat, contenting himself with the bits she did not want. They finished eating and sat looking down across the cold blue of the valley.

From the timber above burst a grey shadow followed by three more. Lobo and his sons had smelled the kill. They descended to dispute the spoils. The king wolf ran ahead, his jaws flecked with foam and his eyes ablaze. At his heels raced his pack, hungry and gaunt, ready to kill and rip to shreds anything that could be eaten.

Bart leaped to his feet and whirled to face the charge. Lobo saw him but did not swerve. With a guttural burst of rage he hurled himself upon Bart. Bart sprang to meet the charge with a howl of defiance. The two great brutes crashed together and went down ripping at each other's throats.

The grey mate did not turn tail. She leaped straight at the first of the dog wolves and fastened her fangs in his throat. The other youngsters sprang to their brother's rescue and the she-wolf went down.

Bart hurled Lobo from him and leaped upon the big dog wolf with a snarl of fury. Lobo side-stepped and slashed out ripping Bart's shoulder in a long gash. Bart twisted about and charged again. This time they closed, rising on their hind legs and slashing at each other's throats. Bart thrust his jaws past the ripping fangs of the wolf and gripped the leader's throat. Lobo wrenched sidewise and shook himself with every ounce of power he possessed, but he could not loosen the death grip that had settled at his windpipe.

The grey one had not fared so well. She had three husky dog wolves upon her. Hunger maddened, seeing red and tasting blood for the first time in many days, they committed the crime of attacking a female of their own kind. She struggled to free herself, to leap back from the fangs that tore at her shoulders and hams but she could not struggle to her feet. She was too weak to save herself and a choked cry of fear was forced from between her teeth.

Bart heard that cry and shook Lobo savagely. With a mighty twist of his powerful shoulders and neck he hurled the leader from him and leaped upon the dog-wolves. He descended upon them like a gory fury, his jaws open and his ears flattened. Leaping into the midst of the murdering trio he slashed and tore. The youngsters whirled upon him and fought back.

Bart ripped one of the pack across the chest as he hurled him aside, then sprang upon the second. He was throttling the third when Lobo leaped upon him from behind and bore him to the ground. The sons took courage as the dog went down and closed in to help finish the fight, but Bart was up and at Lobo's throat with a howl that made the snowbound ridges ring.

There in the cold starlight in the shadows of the spruce Bart showed what a heart he had and what his heritage of killing ancestors had given him. He sent Lobo smashing back upon his haunches and whirled to meet the pack. Hurling the nearest youngster to the ground he leaped back upon Lobo. The old king wolf was the one he must kill. Lobo leaped aside before Bart's rush. He had no desire to feel those iron jaws clamp upon his throat again.

The pack circled and backed off leaving the two foes to face each other. In the snow a yard away lay the she-wolf, motionless and still, Bart leaped upon his adversary again and Lobo broke into a hurried retreat. Bart sent him charging down the slope, but did not follow far. A great fear was clutching at his heart. He must return to the still form in the snow. The pack spread out and took up Lobo's trail.

Bart ran to where his mate lay and nosed her shoulder. She did not whimper and his muzzle came away wet with cold blood. Bart whined and growled, but the grey one did not answer. Already her torn form was stiffening. She had ceased to worry about the hard winter that lay ahead.

The big dog trotted a few yards up the slope, rumbling coaxingly in his throat. When his mate did not stir he returned and tried to get her up. Finally he sat down beside her and waited in silence. Perhaps she was just weak and tired, and asleep. Soon she would waken and they could go back to the cave at the foot of the Engelmann where he could lick her wounds. Midnight came but the grey one lay still.

Dawn came cold and clear to the high country. In a little meadow several miles below Chimney Rock the first light broke over two forms, a grey one and a darker one, lying in the snow. The dark form got up and stood, looking about.

Bart came close to fear as he stood in the new light of day and watched over his dead mate. His wolf instinct told him that with the dawn they should be going, seeking shelter; and his dog instinct told him that he would have to go on alone. It was then that he thought of his old master, remembered the cabin above. When he was troubled and torn by the two instincts that warred within him, he always thought of Sioux Charlie.

With a whimper he broke into a run and headed for the spruce timber and cover. He was running alone, facing the wild as one of its own children, but still no part of it. On through the timber he raced—not looking for food, not interested in his destination, but simply letting his passion and his sorrow play out through his powerful legs. For hours he ploughed through drifts and swung across wind-swept ridges, running on and on.

That night found him far up in the high country and the deep snow had begun to hamper his running. He was tired and hungry and in an ugly mood. Circling along a hog-back he looked down and saw a half dozen cows huddled in a little park. They had been caught by the first snow and had yarded up in an aspen grove. Bart swung down the ridge, his eyes blazing. Somehow he blamed these domestic animals for his trouble. They were a part of the man things he had been forced to avoid since taking to the wilds.

The cows saw him coming and milled about in their tramped paddock. So far they had not suffered much from hunger, and were lively enough to be afraid of the great brute that rushed down upon them.

Bart leaped through a clump of brush and cleared a fallen log. A long strip of cloth tied to a sapling slapped him full in the face and he leaped back as a familiar odor struck his sensitive nose. Sioux Charlie had found those yarded cows and had hung out wolf guards until he could get word down the mountain.

The big dog circled and approached from the far side of the grove. He found a strip of old shirt hanging from a limb on that side, too. Backing off he sat down. His rage had been cooled, and he wanted to wait for a little before attacking the herd in the padded lot. His early training flashed to the fore and he felt again that raging fight within himself, the two instincts striving to win him over.

Stars came out one by one and Bart did not move. He was at one moment a guardian of those cows and the next their mortal enemy, ready to tear one of them down and slash it to ribbons.

A fringe of clouds spread over the rim of Chimney Rock and the wind rose. The spruce on the ridge above the grove whistled and sighed. Bart stirred uneasily. The temperature had gone up and a soft feeling was in the air. The curtain of clouds widened and swept low over the ridge. Then, with a suddenness that was like the closing of a door, the storm descended upon Bart and the cows.

For an hour the snow fell in swirls and gusts driven by an even wind. Then the wind lulled and burst out again with a fury that made the spruce shriek and sent the eddies of white roaring through the naked aspens. Winter had come to the high country with a vengeance and Chimney Rock Mesa was in the grip of a blizzard.

Bart bared his teeth and snapped at the sizzling flakes as they were whipped into his face. The heavy scruff about his neck whitened and froze stiff. A black wall shut out the paddock below him. Bart moved down to the windward of the grove and dug into the snow. He would not run any more that night. He would wait for the storm to break. He was not hungry for food and his rage had cooled. Even the power and rush of the storm raised no answering leap of exultation within him.

CHAPTER XII

Sioux Charlie Returns

SIOUX CHARLIE made several trips down along the frozen creeks and set his traps in all the likely runs and cross runs. He expected to make a catch of marten and coyote with a number of mink and weasel in the smaller sets. The coyote traps were baited with rabbit and the other traps were blind trail-sets or held the lure of a frozen fish.

He also placed some balls of fat on weeds and bushes that stuck up out of the snow. Those balls of fat were to tempt hungry coyotes who would find the hunting hard when the storms hit.

Charlie had discovered a bunch of Circle Bar cows yarded up in an aspen grove and had hung out clothing strips to scare away any band of wolves that might stumble upon them. To Charlie "any band" meant

Lobo and his pack with Bart at their head. He had not sighted the pack but he had seen their tracks once and was almost certain Bart was with them and at their head. The trail he had found had been old and snowed in so he could not be sure. He knew, though, that the big dog was in the country because of these visits paid to his cabin.

The hunter packed some beans and bacon and loaded his snowshoes on his back. He ran a few of his traps on the way down the mountain, then headed for Parsons' home in the valley to tell him about the cows. It would be possible to sled in a bale or two of hay to keep the cows alive till they could be led out, and Charlie saw in this a chance to even himself with the ranch boss for his failure as a hunter.

He slung his rifle over his shoulder and plodded along, ready to go into action in case a wolf or coyote should break cover.

The snow was not yet deep enough for snowshoes so he had to carry them strapped to his back. He would cache them well down the slope and get them on his return. This was Charlie's insurance against a sudden storm.

Charlie plodded along without swerving from a direct course until he struck the rolling foothills. Here he cached his webs—as the mountain men call their snowshoes—in a clump of cedars and dwarf oaks. Strik-

ing out with a light load, he soon reached the Circle
Bar home ranch.

Parsons was the only man at the ranch; the boys were
all out working or in town when Charlie arrived. Parsons welcomed his trapper warmly. He had been afraid
the breed had left the country, and Parsons would never
have rested easy as long as he had Sioux Charlie's savings. He knew the hunter had tried his best to clear the
range. He knew, too, that wolves like the famous white
wolf of the Dakotas or Mountain Billie of the Butte
country had harrassed ranchers for as many as ten years
without being killed. Parsons had felt a little guilty
because he had pressed Charlie so hard.

"Come in and warm yourself," he cried as Charlie
stood in the doorway, his dark face unmoved by any
trace of emotion or welcome.

"I have found six cows in yard up in the breaks at
the foot of the Rock," Charlie said, jerking off his
thick woolen cap.

"So that's where you've been," Parsons cut in.

Charlie nodded and sat down on the edge of the
chair Parsons shoved out for him.

"I have been looking for you, Charlie. Your money
is in the bank to your credit. Don't ever try a trick like
that on me again." Parsons spoke grimly, but there
was a twinkle in his eye. "I want you to stay with the
job and get that pack. Seen anything of them?"

"They are staying close with the rough country and will till they have to come down. That Lobo and Bart know the pack of pups are too green to hunt down here. They stay up maybe all winter, but if they come down it will be no good." Charlie produced his pipe, which was a sure indication that Parsons had eased his mind greatly.

"Now about those cows. Can we get to them with horses?" Parsons spoke slowly. Six cows at the current beef prices meant a lot of money.

"We can get the hay to my place by horse. There we turn the horses loose because she will storm like fury mebby day after tomorrow. From the cabin we pack some hay up and work the beef down." Charlie finished this long speech and lighted his pipe.

Parsons knew from this brief report just what the situation was. The cows were yarded in deep snow and hay would have to be hauled to Charlie's cabin and left there to keep the animals alive until they could be brought out by shoveling and slow breaking of trail.

"If we hit right out today we may be able to get them down to where we can herd them out through the lighter snow. It would be safe to leave our horses a few miles below your cabin wouldn't it?" Parsons asked.

Charlie thought for some minutes then answered.

"I think we take in the hay then take the horses back down to where they will be safe." He spoke between puffs.

Parsons nodded. "I have no men here to send, so I'll go with you myself. Where is your cabin?"

"In West Fork Creek close to the Rock." Charlie always called Chimney Rock, "the Rock."

Parsons got to his feet and busied himself in getting ready for a hard trip. "Get yourself some coffee and open some beans. There is a quarter of beef hanging in the cooler outside the back door," he called from his bedroom.

Charlie proceeded to stir about the kitchen and prepared a meal for both of them. He knew better than Parsons that they might need that full meal before they got so far as his cabin.

"You take webs," he called to Parsons as he poured a brown stream of beans into a frying pan.

"I hate to work in webs, but I'll take them," Parsons promised. He appeared at the door of his room clad in heavy boots and a mackinaw shirt. Charlie surveyed him critically and nodded approval.

"You take six gun, only. I have rifle," he said briefly.

The meal was eaten in silence for the sake of speed. They had no time to waste in conversation. Charlie used a spoon on his beans and scooped up every one before he pushed back his plate.

"The boys can wash up the dishes when they come in tonight. We will rig up a sled and load some bales on it and be going." Parsons reached for his sheep-lined coat as he spoke.

The sled was made ready and packed with hay and some grub and an ax. Parsons' snowshoes were strapped to a bale by Charlie. He looked at the webs and shook his head.

"The gut is rotten and they are warped," he grunted.

"They're good enough for me," Parsons grinned. "I hate to walk on the things anyway."

"Sometimes it is webs or no going," Charlie said shortly.

"I don't look for a bad snow." Parsons jerked a strap tight and prepared to start.

The going was good for seven miles; then it became slower as they struck the deeper snow. The men walked. They led the two horses hitched to the wide-runner sled. The sled had been built for just such expeditions and looked more like a toboggan than anything else. It was light and could easily be hauled by two men if not too heavily loaded. Now it was so well weighted with its five bales of hay and the supplies that the horses were needed to draw it.

Seven miles up a mountain on a steep grade will take a man a great distance in actual climbing. They came to the clump of oaks where Charlie had left his snowshoes and grub, and the hunter's pack was strapped to the sled. Then they ploughed on.

Charlie kept his eyes upon the cold skyline above Chimney Rock. He would know when the storm signs became sure. A storm was brewing, but he could not time it and this made him uneasy. Parsons ploughed along, his thoughts on the work back at the ranch, and on the problem of getting the yarded cows down in safety.

As the snow deepened they halted occasionally to blow their team. Darkness, then starlight, came and still they plodded upward. Charlie had miscalculated their time a little and he was worried. By nine o'clock they broke over the rim of West Fork Canyon and plodded along its narrow bed.

At Charlie's cabin they pulled some hay from one of the bales for the horses and tied them in the shelter of the spruce beside the cabin.

"Think it will be safe to wait till morning to take them down?" Parsons asked.

Charlie had been standing in the open staring up at the starlit sky. He turned and nodded. "I think yes," he said slowly. "But I may not be sure."

The two men stamped to the cabin door. Charlie bent and looked in the snow for tracks. The tracks were there, massive and heavy. Charlie grunted but said nothing. He was thinking deeply, however.

That night the two men rolled themselves in their blankets immediately after a heavy supper of black coffee, sour dough biscuits and fried beefsteak. Charlie lay awake for some time, and listened, but he did not hear the howl he had been expecting, so he dropped off to sleep. Bart was at that moment lying with his nose muzzled across a stiff grey form in an open meadow far down the slope.

Parsons was a lighter sleeper than Charlie and was wakened by the wind howling about the cabin. He rose and threw some big knots into the stove, then went to the door. As he jerked it open, he was met by a roaring blast of snow-filled air. Hastily he slammed the door shut and turned to Charlie. Shaking the sleeping hunter he shouted:

"The storm has broken, Charlie!"

Charlie rolled over and sat up, wide awake; tossed aside the blankets and went to the door. He did not open it wide—only a slit to test the air and the fineness of the driven snow.

"We loosen the horses and let them drift. This may break in the morning and it may not." Charlie was pulling on his heavy coat as he spoke.

"They will go down before the storm all right. We can't have them snowed in, too," Parsons had to shout to make himself heard above the howling of the storm.

The two men stepped outside and loosed the horses.

They led them down the slope for perhaps a hundred yards and sent them drifting into the night. The return trip against the tearing, snow-filled blasts was a staggering one. The wind whipped the breath from their mouths and almost hurled them backward. Inside the cabin Parsons shook the snow from his coat and panted.

"If this doesn't break, we'll lose those cows sure."

"She will break likely," Charlie promised. "For a day anyway."

"How about your trap lines?" Parsons was hugging the stove though its sheet-iron sides were glowing.

"They will wait," Charlie said, pulling off his coat.

The men sat for a time before the stove listening to the howling of the storm. Then they rolled themselves in their blankets again, and let the wind put them to sleep.

Like a grey fury the king wolf closed

CHAPTER XIII

Lobo Hunts

WHEN Lobo led his sons away from the little meadow where he had fought with the great dog he was in a raging mood. Never before had he met a dog that could stand before him for even a brief battle. Many times he had led a pack of hounds into the broken country keeping just ahead of them until he reached a cut bank or a cliff. When he had right flank and rear protection he would whirl and finish them as they came, slashing them to ribbons or hurling them over the cliff. But this great wolf-dog was different; he fought wolf wise and with a viciousness that was not to be stopped.

Lobo limped and his neck was matted with blood but he struck out into the starlight at the head of his pack as though nothing had happened.

Far down the slope a dog coyote saw him pass with his sons at his heels and he shrank into the shadow of a clump of spring willows. In shoving back into the willows he brushed against something that interested him and he forgot Lobo. Sticking to a slender limb was a tempting ball of fat. The coyote was a young one and he was hungry. He sniffed the bait and tasted it with his tongue. It was good. He licked his lips and opened his mouth. Something held him back but he overcame it and bolted the ball of bait.

Having finished this unexpected morsel of food the coyote looked down the slope to make sure Lobo was gone, then he trotted into the open to look for more bits of fat. He did not trot far. The ball of fat melted and its contents sent gripping pains through the young dog. He swayed and staggered, struggling to go on, afraid to lie down, but unable to keep his feet. With a snarling moan he stretched out on the snow within a hundred yards of where Charlie had placed the bait.

Down the slope Lobo was making a wide circle and swinging back up the mountain. He had picked up the trail of an ancient buck, a monarch of the rugged country making his last trip down country. The big fellow had delayed and dallied, his stiff limbs keeping him from striking out until now, when he was forced to go by the approaching storms.

The king wolf sent a hunting call, short and sharp,

ringing into the starlit air and swung down the trail,
cutting back toward the lower country again. Across the
hillside the buck heard the call and struck out as fast
as his stiff joints would carry him.

The pack leaped ahead in full cry, their muzzles low
and their powerful shoulders working as they ran. The
scent began to get hot and Lobo snapped a snarling
order into the wind. At once one of the pack cut off at an
angle and raced down a ridge to the south.

Though still ahead of them, the buck had sighted
his pursuers and burst into a jerking series of leaps
that carried him down the hill faster than the pack. He
was heading for open going on a southern ridge where
he knew he could outdistance his pursuers even though
he was slow as buck speed is reckoned. Swinging away
from his direct course he bounded on. The ridge was
just ahead and he had a safe lead on the charging pack.

As he broke out on the wind-swept hog-back he
swerved suddenly to the right. He had been too dull,
too old to be cunning. Ahead of him rose the grinning
jaws of a grey wolf. One of the pack had cut across to
the ridge and headed him off. The buck whirled and
tried to escape back up the mountain. Like a grey fury
the king wolf closed upon him, hamstringing the monarch with a savage slash. The buck went down but
struggled up again to swing his heavy antlers in a wide
circle. Those sweeping knives did not halt the pack,

they leaped in and were soon snarling and tearing at the quivering carcass.

Lobo was restless, he did not gorge nor did he let the pack gorge, but drove them to the trail again as soon as they had devoured but half the buck. He knew that they could return to the kill and finish it. He was in a savage mood, a killing rage and he wanted new blood. So the pack headed upward, sweeping over the snow like bloody shadows.

They raced on over the crust, spreading and closing again. Finally Lobo halted and growled deep in his throat. His sons halted, too, and sat down to watch what they knew was to be something different. The scruff along the king wolf's back rose and he edged toward a spot in a snow-blanketed cow trail. Whirling he kicked snow and sticks backward viciously. It was evident that he was showing disdain and hatred for something.

His pack watched while Lobo pawed and sniffed and kicked dirt. Had Sioux Charlie seen the proceeding he would have laughed. for Lobo was kicking snow and sticks upon one of his traps and scenting it so that it would be plain to all others of the dog family who might chance that way. Sioux Charlie had seen this happen before and he always laughed; it was one of the few times he would laugh. The joke was always on him in a case of that kind.

Lobo trotted down the hillside looking carefully about. His neck fur rose again and he halted. Lying in the snow a few yards away was a stiffened coyote. Lobo advanced cautiously and stood over the dead coyote. His lips pulled back in a snarl of disdain and he lowered his muzzle. Suddenly he gripped the dog coyote by the neck skin and swung him clear of the ground. Whirling he trotted back up the slope and halted where his pack were resting. With a great heave he hurled the dead body upon the spot where he had been scratching sticks. There was a metallic snap and Sioux Charlie had trapped a dead coyote for the first time in his hunting experience.

The king wolf next raised his muzzle toward the dipper above and howled long and defiantly. His howl ended in a series of calls different from any he had voiced before that night. He sensed a coming storm.

In ten minutes the storm burst over the pack with a fury that shook the spruce above them. Lobo got up and started straight into the fury of the night. He seemed possessed with muscles of steel. His sons joined him and the pack raced through the swirling blizzard.

Lobo halted them on a barren ridge and they all sat down. The wind shrieked across the bare knife-edge of rock and gripped at the grey forms on the ledge. The king wolf lifted his muzzle and began to howl with the storm. His sons joined in and the wind carried a chorus down the slope that would have chilled any man's blood.

And yet the chorus was not unmusical. It had a fearful melody and did not carry that curdling note that always announces blood on the trail when a pack is hunting. Rather the crescendos and the short yelps had a gleeful note. The pack was glorying in the storm, defying it, daring it to sweep them from the ledge. The elements were in a wolf's mood and the pack had in their blood the fury of a band of freebooters.

For perhaps an hour they howled and sang in gleeful abandon, then the leader headed his sons down the ridge and they returned to the carcass of the buck. There in the raging blizzard they tore and snarled and fed. Tomorrow they might be ravenously hungry again but tonight they would be full.

After the bones were stripped and the hide devoured they set out to locate a hiding place against dawn. The day would be spent in sleeping off their full meal. They traveled easily and effortlessly up the mountain. They crossed West Fork below Charlie's cabin and kept on toward patches of aspens on a distant slope that offered deep snow to burrow into.

On the south slope sheltered from the wind the king wolf halted his followers and they burrowed into the snow to let their feast digest.

They burrowed deep and curled up to wait for

another night. The storm passed over them, lulling them to sleep.

Across the ridge on the same slope a great dog was watching a cabin and longing to go down and scratch on the door. When he heard the pack coming across West Fork he returned to a vigil he had set for himself beside a snow-barred lot which sheltered six white-faced cows.

CHAPTER XIV

On Guard

FOR several hours Bart lay with his eyes open while the storm roared above him. In the paddock of snow below the cows were humped over, their backs to the driving sleet and fine snow. Bart could hear them bellow as the blasts of ice cut through their heavy coats of winter hair.

Unable to sleep, driven by a strange restlessness, he rose from the bed he had made and faced into the night. Down the slope he swung breasting into the gale heading toward Chimney Rock. He was sick at heart and lonely. The storm failed to rouse in him that savage mood that comes to all of the dog family when the elements are raging.

He halted for a brief moment on a barren ledge and let the icy particles drive against his teeth. By right he should have been hungry for he had given all his kills to the grey one for many days, and he had fought and run in a way to tax even his great strength. But he was not hungry, for all the gnawing uneasiness within him.

On the ridge that overlooked the little cabin in West Fork Canyon Bart halted and sat down. No light showed below but he knew the cabin was there. He wondered if his old master was still away from home. Getting to his feet he made his way down the slope. He approached the cabin carefully, but in a direct line. At the door he sniffed and listened. Sioux Charlie had returned and some one had come with him. Bart stood for a long time with his head on one side his ears straining.

Within the cabin he could detect even breathing and a great longing swept over him. Lifting a paw he scratched at the door and waited. Suddenly a voice sounded and mingled with the roar of the storm. It was Parsons waking Charlie and telling him of the blizzard.

Bart leaped away from the door and watched while Parsons opened it and looked out. Then he retreated to a spot above the horses and watched Charlie and Parsons come out and lead the animals away. Bart trailed them, keeping well back but always within easy calling distance.

When the men turned the horses loose Bart stood just behind a grey, black curtain of storm and waited.

He waited until the men had turned back. Then he followed them to the cabin. When he saw them enter he whirled and headed down the canyon again. Coming up with the horses he urged them on through the storm. Twice the ponies wanted to halt in the lee of a rock wall but Bart sent them on by snapping at their heels and growling. He was sure Sioux Charlie wanted those horses sent down and he must help.

For five miles he trailed the horses; then left them where the snow was not deep and where they would be able to drift, untempted by sheltering canyons, down to the valleys below. Bart was all dog again, eager to serve his master.

Once the ponies were safe he whirled and headed back toward the cabin. Breasting the storm made him realize that he was weak from want of food, but still he was not hungry. Just below the opening of West Fork Canyon he heard the howling chorus of Lobo and his sons. That howling stirred something within him and he lifted his muzzle. His cry was not like that of the pack. It was the old cry of the killer trained to destroy the freebooters of the range. The wind caught it and hurled it back into his teeth so that Lobo did not hear it, and Sioux Charlie just dozing off in the cabin above did not hear it.

Running on Bart took up a place close to the cabin and sat watching the door. He was crouched thus an hour later when Lobo and his sons passed across the canyon just below the cabin. Bart saw the pack and knew they were headed for the slope where the cows were yarded in. With a snarl he leaped away in a direct line toward that slope.

Bart reached the grove of aspens and juniper and circled about eagerly. He was hoping Lobo would come that way. The storm lessened and the snow became lighter but the pack did not return. Still Bart stood guard watching and waiting. He was determined to guard those cows. Once he had been guardian of the Circle Bar herds and now he had returned to his task. The fight between his wolf nature and his early training had ended with the coming of the storm; now he was all dog.

Bart did not, perhaps could not, put together the events of the summer. He did not know that his return might be unwelcome, that his guardianship might be misunderstood. Nor did he realize that his faithful vigilance would surely be rewarded by a soft nosed ball from Sioux Charlie's rifle if he was found at the paddock. But that is one of the mercies of life among the beasts; they cannot know or think of ends or rewards.

The great dog let his head sink to his paws and dozed off. Though he was still heart-sick over the loss of his mate, and lonesome for the man he loved, like the buck deer, he had no fear until pain came, or loss, or immediate danger. He was spared the worry of wondering what was in the lap of the gods for him.

Morning came with a chill greyness and the storm ceased. Bart walked to the ridge above the snowed-in cattle and sat down. He tested the air and found it still heavy with the promise of more snow and more wind. But for a brief spell the sun broke over a ridge and shed heatless rays upon the driven whiteness of the high country.

Bart watched the ridge below in the direction of West Fork Canyon eagerly. He knew Charlie was an early riser and would be on his way with the breaking of the storm.

Above him an eagle soared and wheeled. Soon another monarch of the air appeared and the two worked along the slope in short spirals, banking and wheeling. They, too, knew that the break in the storm was only for a day at most and were avid with hunting.

Their beating pinions circled about every spruce and pine tree, cutting across each other's path with a whistling swish of air. Their sharp eyes did not miss any of the signs below. They were looking for something that moved, for movement meant life.

They saw Bart lying in the snow but did not give him a second look. Had the big dog been feeding they might have challenged his kill for they were a fierce old pair. But he was resting and they were not interested.

One of them wheeled around a big spruce close to where Bart lay. The beating of the monarch's wings fanned the spruce needles and made them quiver. Within that spruce a blue grouse was perched waiting for a chance to drop down across the snow-bound mountain in search of dried berries and seeds. The darting eyes of the eagle saw the grouse as he shot past and he spread his wings in a steep stall, his tail feathers spreading fanwise. Wheeling he hurled himself at the spruce. He knew that as long as the grouse stayed in the shelter of the spreading boughs it was safe, but he hoped to frighten it out.

The grouse saw his most deadly enemy hurtling down upon him and panic gripped him. In that flurry of fear he did just what the eagle wanted. He launched himself straight out of the tree. With a piercing scream the diving eagle spread himself and checked his drop. Thrashing and screaming he cleared the spruce.

The grouse shot downward at a terrific speed, fear lending his wings momentum. He was a hundred yards down the slope and dropping like a streak before the big eagle that had charged him could clear the spruce.

The fleeing grouse had checked his flight a moment, thinking he had escaped. A pair of talons and a set of piercing eyes cut down through the thin air above. The eagle's mate had been poised above the spruce, waiting. She had folded her pinions and dropped. Her altitude gave her the advantage and her weight shot her earthward like a plummet. The grouse fanned his wings and dived but he was too late. The heavy breast bone of the dropping eagle struck him a crushing blow and he collapsed in a flurry of feathers, tumbling helplessly downward.

Had the pair of eagles been summer hunting or had they been out only for sport they would have left the grouse to lie where he fell; but they were hungry and swooped down to where he lay in the snow. Screaming and clicking their beaks they set upon their feast.

Bart watched this tragedy of the wild without interest. He was all dog, but still not too far removed from the wild nature of his father that he let so common an incident disturb him. He was truly part of this scheme of life that provided for tragedy in its development. Life in the high country is cheap, and fear a passing shadow. Had the grouse escaped he would have forgotten the eagles immediately and gone in search of berries.

The big dog arched his back, rose, and walked down the slope leaving the eagles to their kill. He halted at the edge of the aspen grove and stood looking at the cows. They were a sad half-dozen with their hides stiff with frozen snow. Already their hip bones were shoving through the layers of fat summer feeding had furnished to them.

From his vantage, Bart caught a glimpse of two forms moving slowly upward, but still a great way off. He circled the grove and took a position where he could watch. A great surge of joy filled him. Perhaps it was his master coming. He was still too far for Bart to catch the scent, but he was sure it must be his master. He could see the two men toiling upward, dragging a sled. Across Charlie's back gleamed his rifle and Parsons was packing an ax. The men were on webs and moving very slowly.

Bart was tempted to rush downward to meet them, but the huddled cows in the paddock held him. Lobo and the pack might appear and make a kill if he left. It would take hours for the men to reach the aspen grove; possibly it would be night before they were able to beat their way through.

Bart could not lie down and wait. He ploughed his way through the snow in circles about the yarded cows and watched the men below until they disappeared from sight in a ravine.

CHAPTER XV

Sioux Charlie Shoots to Kill

PARSONS woke first the morning after their arrival at Charlie's cabin. He shook the trapper and both sat up and listened.

"She stop," Charlie said briefly getting out of the bunk.

Parsons swung his feet from under the blankets and reached for his boots. As he pulled them on he blew his breath in a fog toward the stove. "It is colder, Charlie. Possibly the weather will clear for a week or more?" It was more question than statement.

Charlie grunted in answer and began building a fire in the stove that served as both cook stove and heater. He used pine knots to start the blaze and before Parsons had his boots laced the cabin was warm. The pinion knots flamed and roared in the little stove like so much oil. Charlie added a few chunks of balsam and spruce to the fire and began breakfast by washing his face in ice water.

Before he set about making biscuits he went outside where Parsons joined him. The rancher found Charlie looking away past the ragged rim of Chimney Rock. For a full five minutes the Indian looked, then he turned to Parsons:

"We should hurry. The sun she will come up but not for over one day."

Parsons nodded; he agreed with the hunter that the storm was not over. A heaviness was in the air and it had failed to clear brightly and sharply. The sun had not risen yet but there were signs that it would come up in a haze of clouds and shine feebly.

"We better get breakfast over and strike out at once," he said.

Breakfast consisted of hot biscuits, bacon and syrup, with black coffee as a chaser. Both men ate rapidly and in silence. When they had finished Charlie gathered up the dishes and washed them while Parsons went outdoors and cleared the snow away from the sled.

Outside the cabin, Charlie found that Parsons had unloaded all but two bales of hay from the sled and had it pulled up to the door.

"I believe we can drag two bales, but if we can't

we can unload one of them and leave it along the trail.
What do we need to take along?"

"Some grub, your ax and my rifle." Charlie pulled
on his mittens as he enumerated the articles they would
need.

"How about two blankets?" Parsons was looking up
into the haze that hung over the mountains.

"Mebby so two blankets," Charlie agreed. "We likely
stay out all night. If storm she break then we stay out
two nights, mebby three." He smiled one of his rare
smiles and returned inside the cabin.

Parsons slipped on his webs and fitted their straps
tightly. He disliked webs but the heavy snow around
the cabin told him that he would be scarcely able to
move forward at all without them. It was astounding
the amount of snow that had fallen.

Charlie came out with the blankets and a small
pack of food. He had his rifle swung across his arm.
Pulling his webs from a peg beside the door he fitted
them upon his feet. When this was done he slipped the
blankets on the sled over the grub and they were ready
to start.

Charlie broke trail because he was more adept with
snowshoes. He shuffled along in a spraddling walk,
packing the snow into a trail as he went, and pulling his
share of the sled. Parsons was at his heels and strove to
drag a little more than his own share of the load. A half

mile up the side of the ridge Charlie halted and Parsons leaned back against the bales of hay.

"I always said a cowpuncher was no good out of the saddle," he grunted breathing heavily and mopping his brow.

"You get your next wind pretty quick like," Charlie promised.

"I'll break trail," Parsons offered. "And that will get me my second wind."

"You follow me, boss," Charlie said. "It is better that you do what you can than to have you give out."

Parsons saw the sense of this and agreed silently.

The sun mounted the sky in a haze as the men had known it would, but within the course of an hour it had brightened and was shining on the new snow with disconcerting glare.

Charlie looked worried; he had not expected any bright sun. He plodded on breaking trail and driving straight up the slope. He was hoping the haze would settle again and protect their eyes. At last he halted and slipped from his harness.

The halt was made beside a dead spruce and Charlie went over to the rotting tree. He chipped some bark loose and piled it on the snow. Then he took out his matches and lighted the pile of bark. When the tiny fire was going he held a piece of rotten wood in the flames. As soon as the wood was charred Charlie motioned to Parsons, and the ranch boss came over to Charlie's side.

"Rub this under your eyes plenty," the hunter ordered.

Parsons blackened his cheeks under his eyes and looked about. The strain from the glaring snow was lessened greatly and he did not squint so much. Charlie blackened his own cheeks and when he was satisfied with the job on Parsons he returned to the sled. Taking up the harness he waited for the rancher to get in line; then he struck out without a word.

For two miles they ploughed upward steadily until they had reached the rim above the cabin. There Charlie halted and pointed to a far slope. "We go there," he said briefly.

Parsons looked and judged the distance with his eye. "We can't make it before mid-afternoon," he ventured.

"Not then. She snow a foot more than I expect," Charlie answered.

After this brief rest they plunged on again, dropping into a little canyon that wound upward in a twisting course. Every foot of the way cost energy and was gained through hard work. The stops became more frequent and Parsons began to show signs of tiring. Charlie looked at the sun and judged the noon hour to be only a quarter off. Halting, he dropped his harness.

"We eat," he said briefly and suited the words to

action by breaking a handful of dry branches from a wind-torn spruce. A fire was soon crackling and Charlie had snow melting for tea. Black coffee was all right at the cabin but hot tea was the trail stimulant he always used. Parsons lay upon the snow and rested his aching back.

"I hope we can get both bales through." Parsons finally spoke from under the shade of his thick mittens which he had laid across his face. He was experiencing snow burning and his chin and cheeks were beginning to blister. Charlie looked at him and judged that the big blisters on his chin would break before sundown that night. In his own mind he knew that Parsons was due for a sleepless night but he said nothing. His own dusky face was unmarked and his black eyes were as clear as ever.

"It is ready," Charlie announced shifting the tea pot to a bed of dying embers where it would not boil. Charlie had built a fair-sized fire and when it had begun to burn down he had raked the coals out flat and had fried bacon as easily as he might have on the stove in the cabin. Charlie was woods-bred and never built a big fire.

Parsons sat up and took his tin plate eagerly. He swallowed several gulps of the hot tea and felt better. The crisp bacon and some of the biscuits from breakfast filled in and helped the tea to restore his vigor.

After the meal was over Charlie lay back against the trunk of the spruce and closed his eyes. Parsons shaded his face again and the two men lay as though asleep. Charlie got up at the end of half an hour and packed away the tea pot and the frying pan. When he had finished he roused Parsons and they slipped into the harness.

The going was steadily getting steeper and their course wound in and out around patches of spruce and groves of aspens. Chimney Rock showed plainly at their backs but the rim of West Fork Canyon had disappeared from sight. They were in a silent world, a solitude of white expanses broken by the green of the spruce. The aspens stood, scarred and cold, only a shade lighter than the snow. The two men labored upward with their eyes on the ground.

By three o'clock the cold haze of the morning had returned to the mountains and the sun rode coppery grey on a ribbed ridge to the east. Charlie increased his speed and threw more of his weight upon the sled ropes. He was worried by the change in the weather. If it was to be clear on the morrow, the evening should come with crystal brightness and a biting cold that would register thirty or forty below. As it felt now, the temperature was not more than zero.

Parsons had noticed the signs as soon as Charlie. When the hunter increased the pace he steeled his muscles against his growing weariness, and held his harness tight. He was not afraid of a night in the open but he did not anticipate with cheerfulness another blizzard, especially when it might last several days. Parsons was ploughing along with his eyes on the trail-points of Charlie's webs when the hunter ahead of him halted. Parsons looked up to see what the halt was for.

Ahead of them and not a hundred yards along the slope was a clump of aspens. Within the clump was a padded yard-like circle and inside the circle stood six dejected white faced cows. When they sighted the rescue party with the two bales of hay they set up a wild bawling and floundered into the deep snow.

Charlie had seen this and he had seen more, too. He had sighted a big brute of a dog circling around the grove. Like a flash his rifle came down and he set himself for a shot.

Up on the slope the dog had started to circle downward. He had seen the dull flash of the rifle barrel and had floundered back up the hill in a spray of snow. His powerful leaps carried him upward rapidly and he was almost out of sight behind a drift when Charlie's rifle spoke. The dog hurled himself from sight behind the drift but his last ploughing leap left a red trail in the snow.

Charlie lowered his gun and his hands were trembling. He looked long at the drift behind which Bart had leaped, then he swung his rifle to his back. Without looking at Parsons he jerked up on the sled ropes.

"I believe he was watching those cows," Parsons called with a queer note in his voice.

Charlie halted and faced about. "Yes. And he was a killer, that feller. I shoot his mate and he is sorry and would make up. But now I shoot him." There was a bitter light in the hunter's eyes that made Parsons lower his gaze.

"I guess you're right, Charlie," was all he could say.

The rescuers ploughed to the padded yard and cut open one of the bales of hay. They gave the cows part of it and prepared to make camp. The animals would have to be worked down along the trail the men had opened. It would take several days and a lot of hard work.

Charlie made supper and fixed a shelter of spruce boughs with aspen saplings for supports. Parsons insisted on helping him. He cut all the props and the limbs. Parsons was not a woodsman and his awkwardness with a razor-sharp ax made even the stolid Charlie nervous. Finally the Indian took the ax and finished the cutting.

Not until camp had been made and wood gathered for the night did Charlie turn his face toward the drift with the bloody trail across it. Parsons had been watching him closely and felt relieved when the hunter strapped on his webs and headed silently up the slope.

At the edge of the drift Charlie paused and looked down into the snow. The big dog had fallen but he had risen and gone on, fighting in a zig-zag course through the clinging whiteness. Charlie followed the red trail for a little way then turned back. He was sorry not to find a stiff carcass behind the drift.

The hunter returned to camp where Parsons had a fire roaring. He sat down before the blaze and slipped off his mittens. He was sure that he would not see Bart again. The great spots of blood on the trail and the tracks, spasmodic and aimless, left little room for any other conclusion, though Charlie knew that Bart was tough and strong, that he had a heart of iron within him and a frame that was almost shock-proof.

"If he should come back," the Indian muttered— then stopped and reached for the pack of food. "It will storm by morning," he finished deliberately and those were the only words Parsons heard from him until the next dawn.

The two men spread their blankets on spruce boughs under their lean-to shelter and fixed themselves to sleep. Parsons was worn out but his face had blistered and the skin was breaking. The hot water from the blisters ran down his cheeks like liquid fire and he could not sleep. He gritted his teeth and tried not to disturb his companion with his twisting. As the night wore on sheer exhaustion brought rest to the ranch boss. He drowsed with a fitful jerking of his aching shoulders.

While the men slept a great dog was battling with two hurts, both inflicted by the only living thing he cared about. One of the wounds was real and cost him much red blood, the other was a greater hurt and closer to his heart. He was bewildered and sick, but he was not dead. He had crawled back under a shelf of rock that was free from snow and there he crouched licking his torn side.

A heavy blood clot had frozen over the wound preventing continued loss of blood. The big dog did not nurse his wound long; he lay with his massive head on his paws and looked straight out of the cave with unblinking eyes. He was again struggling with those two instincts, and the lure of the trackless wilderness had almost won.

CHAPTER XVI

Blood on the Trail

PARSONS and Charlie were awakened at four o'clock by a howling, roaring wind. They felt fine snow sifting through the shelter and settling on their faces. Charlie tossed aside the blanket and crawled out. He stood up and was almost swept from his feet by a snow-laden blast. Parsons wiggled out with his sheep-lined coat over his head and stood beside the hunter.

"We are in for a tough day," he bellowed into the breed's ear.

Charlie did not reply but he bent and dragged his heavy coat from under the shelter and pulled it on. He felt about in the thick darkness and found his mittens. Putting his lips close to Parsons' ear he shouted:

"We got to fix the cows and make it back to the cabin. This storm she is bad. The hay will last till we can get back up."

Parsons squeezed Charlie's arm by way of reassurance and agreement and bent below the rim of the shelter to keep the stinging blasts from his sore face.

Charlie got to his knees and crawled back under the shelter. "We rest till day light," he shouted pulling the blanket up over his coat.

Parsons followed his example and they lay listening to the storm and waiting for light. They could not sleep, but action in that thick blackness would be useless so they lay still.

The next three hours passed like so many days for Parsons. His face was burning and he was restless to be out fighting the storm. He wondered if the hay they had brought up would last till they could beat a trail back to the cows. He was glad they had made it; otherwise the animals might have starved if they had gone much longer without help.

Charlie lay and thought of other things. The storm did not bother him as a storm, but it did remind him of the great dog he had shot down the afternoon before. Bart had gloried in storms. He had been wild and untamed in his glory when a storm struck. His howl had been the exact duplicate of that of a grey wolf. Charlie had always felt a mad power rise within him when he and Bart were breasting a blizzard together. The big dog had roused it in him and he had liked it.

Both men lay and let their thoughts wander where they would while they waited for daylight. The storm abated not at all. It tore at the shelter and sifted its fine snow down through the boughs into their faces. The wailing of the spruce added a weird note to the turmoil of the elements and colored the pictures that rose in each man's mind.

Daylight came at last and Charlie was the first out. Parsons had dozed off and Charlie let him sleep until he had examined the storm signs. Everything was blotted out except a few grey spruce laden with snow. Charlie made his way past the upturned sled and tried their old trail. It was obliterated in places but he thought he might be able to use it to advantage and to follow it.

Next Charlie set about fixing the hay so that the cows could get it and still not trample it into the snow. When he had finished with that he returned to the shelter and wakened Parsons.

There was no hot breakfast that morning. The two men swallowed cold bacon and biscuit and made ready to start immediately. Charlie rolled two packs, one from each of the blankets. He placed all the food in his pack and left Parsons an empty blanket. Picking up the ax he handed it to the rancher, then he swung his rifle over his shoulder and faced down the slope with the wind. Parsons had finished strapping on his webs and fell in behind Charlie with the ax and his pack on his back. His sense of direction was keen, but he would not have trusted it on a day like this without Charlie up ahead. He could scarcely see the heavy shoulders of the breed a rod before him and was forced to keep close to him.

They ploughed on for two hours with the storm hurtling its fury down upon them. Parsons wondered how Charlie could follow the trail, and Charlie *was* having trouble keeping to their back track. The wind had swept away all but the packed places where their shoes had settled the day before and now the new snow was rapidly covering these marks. Then, too, the storm seemed to be thickening and growing colder. Charlie began to consider making a new camp. If he lost the trail even his keen senses might lead them wrong.

They fought on for another hour. Charlie was stopping frequently now to test the trail and to peer into the storm for familiar spruce trees or other landmarks close to their course. Twice they had floundered away from the old trail and almost lost it. The hunter knew they were facing a situation that was grave but he shoved on again after a five minute search revealed the trail. The course now quartered into the wind and soon they were facing full into the fury of driven ice and snow. Charlie could no longer depend on his eyes to tell him where they were going; he had only the hard pressure of the packed sled trail to guide him as his webs moved ahead.

They fought their way at last to a wind swept hogback. There Charlie found no trail at all but only a packed and glazed crust of old snow. He tried to place his course, to strike the trail on the far side of the hogback and worked on across the ridge. He was almost ready to face about, heading back to the shelter they had used the night before but he was afraid the storm might last longer than their food.

As they reached the top of the hog-back they felt the full fury of the storm and were forced to bend low to make any headway. Dropping down on the far side of the rim they struck patches of timber again and Charlie began to look for the trail. He mushed first to the right and then back to the left along the timber line and close in where the snow was deep. His webs ploughed along with a steady and silent spurting of snow but they failed to strike the trail of the day before. Charlie halted and waited for Parsons.

Parsons came up slowly. He was a poor hand with snowshoes and already his back was aching from the spraddled position he was forced into in order to walk. Charlie bent close to him and shouted:

"The trail she is gone."

Parsons did not reply for some minutes. He was

looking the situation squarely in the face and weighing their chances. Finally he shouted. "Had we better try to camp?"

"We should camp and hope for a break," the hunter bellowed.

Without waiting for Parsons to agree Charlie plunged downward in search of a spruce grove. After five minutes of going a ghostly outline of white and green showed through the wall of hurtling ice and they mushed into a circle of trees. The green boughs broke the wind and made the snow eddy and swirl down upon them as though from a great sifter.

Parsons swung the ax from his shoulder and began looking for wood. He was beginning to chill with the intense cold. Coming from the lower valleys where Indian summer was in its softest mood he was scarcely able to stand the sudden change. He found a dead spruce and began slashing limbs from it with the ax.

Charlie had pulled out his hunting knife and was attacking the green boughs, preparing to make a shelter. He tramped a round spot in the snow and tossed the branches into it.

Parsons had cleaned the tree of branches to a height equal to his head and was looking for limbs lower down. Kicking the snow aside he bared a thick limb that had fallen from the tree. It was embedded in the snow and he swung the sharp ax and slashed at it. His back was to

The great dog shot through the air

the dead spruce and the arc of the ax made it graze the trunk. The keen blade was deflected and shot downward out of line with the limb in the snow. There was a sickening thud and Parsons' fingers went numb. A stabbing pain shot through his right leg and blood spurted to the snow.

"Charlie!" Parsons shouted. "Come here!"

Something in the boss' voice made the hunter leap to his side. He looked down and saw the blood. Kneeling he jerked off his mittens and pulled aside the slashed boot flap from the calf of Parsons' leg. The wound was an angry one, spurting blood intermittently. Charlie's mask-like face did not change but he rose and pulled Parsons toward the pile of boughs he had been heaping up.

"It is an artery," he shouted as he forced Parsons down upon the spruce needles. For five minutes he worked, tearing strips from his shirt and making a loop high up on Parsons' leg. Into the loop he forced a stick and twisted as hard as he dared. The blood flow lessened but refused to stop. Charlie wrapped bandages and jerked them tight in an attempt to stop the flow of blood but each bandage spotted and spread in a red stain a few seconds after he placed it.

Charlie rose and stood looking down at his friend. Parsons was white as the snow about him except for the hollows under his eyes. These were purple. Charlie knew what that meant, Parsons was chilling and he was growing weak. The trip had taxed him severely and the loss of blood was telling on him. Charlie realized that he had a very sick man on his hands and he also realized that his trail was lost. Bending over he shouted:

"We have to go on, feller, like we been. You must be at the cabin soon. I have medicine and lime there to stop the blood."

Parsons nodded up at him and tried to haul himself to his feet.

"It should not be far to the cabin. We crossed the canyon rim back a way," he answered gritting his teeth to keep back a groan.

"It is not far. The cabin she is just below." Charlie spoke the truth but he did not add that he could not go to the cabin because he had missed the trail and his bearings in the lashing maelstrom that was tearing at the spruce above them.

Tossing aside his rifle and the ax he pulled one of Parsons' arms over his shoulder and started off. Charlie had been forced to remove the rancher's webs and Parsons sank deep into the loose snow. Slowly they ploughed their way out of the grove and into the teeth of the wind. The tracks Parsons made in the snow showed red stains in little patches.

Charlie did not look back. He was grimly trusting to luck and hoping that some familiar landmark would show through the white wall of fury that was tearing down upon them. They struggled on for perhaps a half mile. Parsons went limp and Charlie had to stop and revive him by applying snow to his lips and forehead.

Parsons smiled grimly as he came to and straightened up. He was game to the last and refused to quit. "Let's get going, Charlie," he said through clenched teeth. The wind whipped the words from his mouth and obliterated them, but Charlie read their meaning plainly. Gripping the weakened man's shoulders he pushed on, half-carrying, half-shoving his burden.

They moved along slowly, painfully. Parsons was growing numb from the cold. His leg seemed to be losing its searing pain and he was growing drowsy. Charlie shook him and jerked him forward. The hunter was afraid of what the next half hour would bring forth. No familiar trail sign had showed. They might be within a quarter of a mile of the cabin or they might be hopelessly far away from it, above or below. One thing was certain, they had reached the bed of West Fork Canyon. Now he must decide whether to go up or down.

Charlie chose to go up and faced that way. He was almost carrying Parsons now and could move only at a dragging walk. Fifty feet of going ended Parsons' efforts, he wilted and sagged, a dead weight on Charlie's shoulders. The wounded leg stained the snow red as it sank deep into a drift.

The hunter let his friend down and began rubbing and pounding him to get the circulation started again. It would never do to let Parsons drowse off in a semi-conscious condition or he would freeze to death.

Working rapidly he fought for his friend's life though he feared in his heart that they would both lie there to be found in the spring. Possibly they would be discovered by one of the Circle Bar's own riders within the shadow of the cabin. Charlie never once thought of leaving Parsons and setting out alone. He knew that to do so might mean he could never find Parsons again.

CHAPTER XVII

The Pack Closes In

LOBO and his sons slept through the sunshine of the day after the first storm. When the second storm burst across the slopes below Chimney Rock they crawled out of their snow beds and shook the frost from their manes. Lobo was ready to fare forth again and the pack was hungry.

The fury of the elements tuned the wolves to a high pitch as they fought through the deep snow down across the ridges. Lobo plunged ahead leaping over drifts and driving through the swirling blasts of ice. His jaws were spread in a snarl and he slashed out at the biting sleet and snow as he drove along.

His sons ran almost abreast of him. They were not hoping to pick up a trail or flush any game that night;

they were running with a wild defiance of the storm. If they crossed a trail they would kill, as much to satisfy their mood, as for their hunger, which was great.

Swinging into a ravine the pack swept up its far side and crossed a wind cleared ridge. Their toe nails bit into the crust where they ran, and each muzzle was raised in a yelping howl. Over the rim they leaped and down into the deeper snow along the fringe of timber below. Two of the pups swung through a clump of spruce which Lobo skirted. A sudden howling and snarling rose. Lobo whirled to join his pack. He leaped into the spruce cover, his muzzle close to the trail.

Within the swirling snow of the sheltered grove the king wolf found his two sons nosing a fresh trail. With a snarl he leaped forward and sniffed. His mane rose and he lifted his massive head to the storm. The call he hurled into the grey fury was long and deep. It meant "blood on the trail." The third youngster came leaping to the pack as he heard that call.

With eager yelps the pack took up the marked trail and rushed away down the mountain. No matter that the trail held man scent, there was blood on it and that was enough. Lobo took the lead and leaped away with a fury that equalled the storm.

The trail was filling with snow, but the wolves had no trouble following it. At every rise Lobo hurled his hunting call into the wind as he raced on.

Down in the canyon Charlie heard the cry and his lips drew tight as it flashed upon him that he had thrown away his gun and the ax. He tried to rouse Parsons but the rancher was unconscious. Charlie looked about and finally found a spruce limb. Sitting down he placed this across his knees and waited. He would make an accounting of himself when the pack arrived. He knew they were on the blood-marked trail. Lobo's howl had told him that.

The pack swept downward eager for a kill, their noses telling them that the end of the trail was not far ahead. Lobo had allowed all caution to be carried away on the blasts of the storm. These were his enemies. He leaped forward.

The hunting cry of the killers floated back upon the wind and was caught by the quick ears of a lone dog who was struggling to cover with his last strength. Bart felt he must reach the cabin in West Fork Canyon before the burning pains in his side finished him. He heard the cry of the pack and though he swung in behind them, it was because they were heading toward the cabin he sought. He did not try to overtake Lobo. His hatred of the great wolf was dulled by his weakness.

Leaping along he picked up the trail and loped slowly down it, his face set high into the storm.

Lobo and his pack burst upon Sioux Charlie and his charge with a fury that made the storm seem tame. As the wolves sighted the two men they spread out and charged. Lobo paused only long enough to make sure the men had no guns, and when no deadly report came from the stick Charlie held, Lobo leaped forward.

Charlie sprang to his feet and swung his club above his head. The pack split and whirled past him to wheel and swing in a wide circle around the two men. Slowly the circle narrowed and the snarling pack closed in. Parsons was roused by the howling and got to his knees. Jerking off his mittens he prepared to meet the first attack with his bare hands.

The pack shifted their circling and halted. Lobo gathered himself and bolted downward. Charlie shouted and swung his club, and the leaping wolf was caught across the muzzle but he crashed in without slowing. Charlie ripped out his hunting knife and the man and the wolf went down.

Charlie's shout was heard back on the trail by a weary dog who was making his way home. The shout seemed to transform the slow loping dog. He halted and his muzzle dropped to the trail for the first time. Then it raised and a howl came from the great chest. Bart was answering his master's cry.

Down on the floor of the canyon Charlie heard that cry and he slashed at the bristling, tearing jaws above him with a wild hope springing in his heart. If Bart could make it in time! Charlie never doubted that the dog was coming. In that hour of danger he knew that Bart was true to him.

Bart thrust upon the scene of the battle just as the pack leaped upon Parsons. They had held back to see how Lobo fared with the man he attacked. Now that their leader had hurled the hunter to the snow they closed in.

The great dog shot through the air like a screaming shell and landed with crushing force on Lobo's back. His teeth sank into the shoulder of the wolf and there was a crushing of bones. Lobo was bowled over leaving Charlie lying in the snow.

Charlie's heavy coat with its sheepskin collar had saved him. He had pulled his head down into the collar and the fangs of the wolf had not torn through. Leaping to his feet the hunter sprang upon the pack around Parsons. His knife sank into the side of one of the whelps and the wolf staggered back mortally wounded. The other two leaped aside snarling and yelping.

Charlie charged them and they sprang back into the deep snow.

Bart and Lobo were rolling over and over. The king wolf was attempting to hurl that slashing demon from him, to use his deadly tactics of slashing and leaping back, but the deep snow made him stand and fight. No wolf could have stood before the onslaught of Bart that day. He crushed the wolf down into the snow and set a viselike grip upon his throat.

The burst of fury that had carried him into the fight ebbed as soon as it had come, but it did not ebb until Lobo went limp under his jaws. The two great beasts collapsed together in the snow. Bart lay motionless, his jaws set like iron clamps while Lobo's upturned legs still jerked spasmodically.

Charlie bent over Parsons once he had routed the young wolves. The man was conscious though badly scratched and slashed about the face. Charlie lifted him up and Parsons opened his eyes.

"They didn't get us?" he asked feebly.

"Bart, he come," Charlie said briefly and there was a choked sound to his voice that the storm could not drown.

Parsons sat up and looked around. He saw Bart lying in the snow with his jaws set at Lobo's throat. He motioned for Charlie to go to his dog.

Charlie went eagerly. He bent over and looked down upon his one-time pal. Lobo's jaws were gaping wide and his eyes bulged. Suddenly Charlie bent lower and a shout burst from his lips. Jerking Bart loose from the wolf he pulled the dog's head to him and rocked back and forth.

It was the rocking or possibly the Indian words Charlie was saying that wakened Bart. He opened his

eyes and his jaws parted in a grin of welcome. Weakly
he attempted to get up but Charlie held him tight.

After a time the hunter stood and dragged Bart to
his feet. Together they turned to Parsons who was
sitting in the snow.

"Lobo, he have a broken fang, too, like Bart,"
Charlie shouted. "Bart is good dog. I see it now, all
of the things he did." The hunter's face had lost its
mask and was shining. "Bart, he know the way to the
cabin. Home, Bart, we go home." Charlie waved his
arms into the storm.

Bart uttered a growling rumble deep in his chest
and faced up the canyon. Charlie pulled the other man
to his feet. Charlie could not put his own webs on again
for the straps had broken under the strain of Lobo's
charge, and, too, he must help Parsons along.

Slowly the three ploughed their way up the canyon.
Bart staggered ahead, but for all his weakness he was
eager and happy. After going for less than a half mile
the cabin appeared out of the white wall of storm.

Charlie opened the door and the first to enter was
Bart. It was truly a prodigal's return. Charlie fixed
Parsons' leg and built a fire, then he dressed Bart's
wound. This done he began preparing food for them all.

From his place on the bunk Parsons called to Charlie
who was cutting bacon at the little plank table: "That
dog has heart enough for both of us and some to spare."

Charlie nodded happily and tossed Bart a slice of bacon. The slice was not rind, as it used to be in the old days. It was fat with a streak of lean, the choicest cut on the slab.

That night Bart slept, after eating his first food since the death of the grey one. He slept as of old with his head close to the foot of Charlie's bunk. His wound had sunk to a mere nothing. He would pay no attention to it from now on. He was right with his little world again. Lobo, his enemy, lay drifted under by the driving storm with the pack scattered and one of them killed. But the greatest victory of all was his vindication in the eyes of his master.

Sioux Charlie lay sleeping with a smile on his face. He was cleared in the mind of the man who had trusted him and he was happy. When the storm broke he and Bart would go up to rescue the yarded cows, while Parsons rested in camp until his leg was well. Then they could go down to tell the ranchers how the hunter, Sioux Charlie, had won out. His dog and he would hunt together again, trusting each other and trusted by their friends.

Charlie slept more soundly than he had in many nights.

[THE END]